Inside The Flavor League
A Slightly Buzzed Satirical Novel

BY

Paul Moser

Inside the Flavor League
Copyright © 2016 by Paul Moser

Published in the United States and the United Kingdom by Venial Press

ISBN 978-0-9847941-4-0 (pbk.)

First edition 2016

Printed in the United States of America
Cover Design: Kirk Henderson

Thanks to Meghan Pinson and Sunny Cooper for Developmental Editing

1 2 3 4 5 6 7 8 9 10

"…many triumphs of justice are mockeries of law."
—Thomas Hardy

"Enjoy our products responsibly."
—Multishots USA

*With gratitude
to the iconic culture commandos, the Firesign Theatre:
Phil Austin, Peter Bergman, David Ossman, and Phil Proctor*

"Just because you're surrounded by evil doesn't
mean you can't make some money from it."

TABLE OF CONTENTS

Inside The Flavor League

INTRODUCTION: OUT OF THE SHADOWS

With so many pieces of the Flavor League story surfacing in the media, I've got to admit the obvious: This book is late to the party. I can just hear Dion, League chairperson and aficionado of old pop music, quoting from the 1958 hit song "Born Too Late" by the Poni-tails:

> Born too late to have a chance to win your love

But here's the thing: this book *can* win your love. In a face-off with those trashy, rush-to-publish Flavor League histories already on the market, it's no contest—unless you're someone who actually enjoys sloppy reportage and knuckle-dragging syntax. If that's what floats your boat, then sure, you might be happy reading potboilers penned by poseurs and conspiracy theorists who take a smattering of research from police reports in a few cities around the world and blend it with just enough wild-ass speculation to create a pile of journalistic junk food.

But if you're craving hard-hitting inside information, real stories of League heroes and their struggles with unremitting evil in the marketplace of potable alcohol, then you're ready for *Inside the Flavor League*. It delivers exclusive information available only through primary sources and tireless scholarly research—not just through a powerful talent for making shit up. My sixteen years as the League operative known as Vinnie, as well as my subsequent years spent documenting the League's apparent demise and resurrection, make me uniquely qualified to write not just about its most pivotal historical moments, but also about the lives of its most distinguished members.

Let me sketch out the landscape for you, before we plunge in.

The Flavor League was founded for one reason only: to bring justice to the murky, sleazy, down-and-dirty world of wine and spirits. We were dedicated to the kind of decisive, cut-to-the-chase, real-world justice that people everywhere pine for, but that official agencies charged with the task never seem to deliver.

In 1975, our tiny group, including experts in fields as diverse as espionage, pharmaceutical research, psychology, logistics, and of course wines and spirits, applied to a variety of agencies with world-wide reach requesting to work under their auspices to stamp out the rampant illegal, unethical, and dickish behavior of powerful wine and spirits interests. Rebuffed by the World Health Organization, which did not accept the claim that ours was a public health issue; by UNESCO, which denied our claim that we were promoting culture through international respect for justice; and even by INTERPOL, which refused support on the flimsy grounds that we were not a bona fide police organization, we were forced to strike out on our own: an anonymous, shadowy group of highly-trained renegades using unorthodox methods to achieve our goals. When critics decried a particular mission we carried out, or a target we neutralized, saying that we were arbitrary or unfair or inconsistent or even dictatorial in our choices, we said: Suck it. So sue us. If you can find us, that is.

Over many years, in a dozen countries, the League carried on its anonymous fight for true justice. Because of obviously delicate legal issues, with the exception of the two subjects of this work whose identities no longer need protection, I have extended, through the use of pseudonyms, the cloak of anonymity to League members mentioned in this tale. I assume they continue the great work even now, scattered around the world, a diaspora of genius and rebelliousness. This book is offered as testimony to their dedication.

So who were our enemies, then? The people we brought to justice? Over time, we found that they were overwhelmingly male. No surprise there. The greater number of them were scumsuckers, bounders, and blackguards, of course. But through careful research, we were also able to identify some number of jagoffs, shitheads, and real pricks among their number. For the most part, they were wealthy and powerful—that is, those who had the means to influence the wine and spirits world, and who, in our judgment, misused that power. Many were producers of wine or spirits; some sold or distributed the products. Some were journalists. Some were notable conspicuous consumers with large collections, or—a special favorite of ours—those who invested in them as "commodities."

The motives of our targets were depressingly transparent. In most cases it was sheer avarice, though nearly 70% of those were more or less tinged with garden varieties of insecurity stemming from bedwetting, absentee fathers, inability to socialize, penis size—that sort of thing. The combination created an insatiable desire for social standing and perceived sophistication. Cultural refinement as a means to respectability and fame. That's just about it. We were constantly on the lookout for deeper motives in our targets, but invariably came away disappointed.

What form did our justice take? That question is a little complicated and needs some historical background, so I hope you will bear with me. I can't just say that we were using a modified Zipp formula, with more and more frequent deployment of MLII; it would mean nothing to you.

When the League was formed, its fourteen charter members decided that lethal force was off the table. But if we weren't willing to liquidate our targets, what punishment was possible that would make a lasting impression on these bastards? A tough issue, and one that was hotly debated for several weeks, until Dion, key pharmacology specialist as well as League chairperson-for-life, presented us with the Gilbert and Sullivan answer that was satisfyingly obvious: the punishment should fit the crime. He suggested that he could synthesize a fast-acting, relatively easy-to-administer drug that would seriously affect the target's sense of taste and smell for extended periods.

Easier said than done, as it turned out. Since we obviously had no willing participants for clinical trials, we had to experiment on identified targets in the field. Working with variations of known psychedelics, Dion put together a few beta drugs to be administered through ingestion. These crude substances ultimately proved unsatisfactory, however, often simply making the target nauseous for a few days, or creating hallucinations which were reportedly not nearly unpleasant enough. Refining his work, Dion created a substance that would scramble the target's taste sensations such that formerly pleasant tastes became disgusting and vice-versa. Because the drug was concentrated and involved heavy metals, it was easy to provide a dose whose effects would last anywhere from one to ten years, depending on the target's body weight and overall health.

The first instances of its use in the field revealed an unanticipated benefit, too. It was discovered that within five minutes of ingestion the target would begin actually to quack, just like a duck, for anywhere from fifteen minutes to two hours. Not only did League members appreciate the embarrassment/humiliation aspect of it, but the response also served as confirmation that the target had indeed been neutralized. Though even Dion had not anticipated this side-effect, he was later able to offer a feasible theory as to how it came to be. He explained in a memo that two of the compounds in the formula were originally used by the Canadian government to sterilize wild ducks that were breeding in unacceptable numbers.

So this, our initial weapon, commonly known as "Flip," was first deployed in 1976. We now refer to it as "Screwball," the ultimate in unintended consequences.

It was used twenty-three times through 1979; and until late 1980 no one in the League was aware of any problems. On the contrary, we thought it was a huge success. Media outlets described a mysterious malady affecting members of the wine and spirits community, one that rendered its victims distressed and anxious from an inability to connect familiar foods and beverages with expected aromas and tastes. We congratulated Dion and each other when these reports surfaced. Yet with the passage of time we couldn't help but notice that many of our targets had not left their professional positions in the wine and spirits world. In fact, they were more in evidence than ever. When we understood that many of the businesses owned or controlled by our targets were fielding some truly awful products, presumably relying on their newly-flawed senses of taste and smell, we were horrified. That we might have triggered this wave of bad taste was our worst nightmare. Some products came far too close to being successful, too, which was especially distressing.

You might remember Gastrima, for example, which débuted at the end of 1979. Flooker Brothers out of New York gave the world this "American Adult Beverage" in a can, with its color of snail flesh, tasting like an electrical fire smells. At about the same time there appeared "Getrunken qba," a German product touted as the new *haupt*-avatar of everyday white wine. Being part of the Bayer empire, it had huge advertising muscle behind it, and a fancy label which included an exquisite medieval woodcut depicting what would later be identified as a witch and her dog asleep under a tree. It was crude, more or less potable sweet wine, but with the added crowd-pleasing feature of glowing in the dark. Possibly the League's most distressing moment was seeing Chateau Boullox, the elite wine producer in Bordeaux's Saint Emilion region, marketing "Tete Violette," the world's first red wine beer, a product whose flavors seemed solidly based in Belgian hops and stomach bile. It was served for almost a year on all Air France business class flights originating in Europe.

Thank God that Dion rose to the occasion then, in

mid-1981, when we were at our most shame-faced and de-moralized. He suggested the way out of the disaster: a drug that would be a variation on Flip—every bit as fast-acting and long-lasting, but whose primary effect would be to rob the target of *all taste or smell* for up to ten years. It took another year and a few false starts, but by mid-1982 the new weapon was being deployed. It would become known as "Zipp" and would become so successful that a third generation of its original formula was still used by many operatives in the fateful year of 1991.

There was another arrow in our pharmacological quiver, too. Formulated in the mid-eighties as a more severe alternative to Zipp, which then came to be used for less vile offenders, there was Molly Liberation, or ML. Its formula, which included a powerful advanced version of the street drug known as MDMA, or Ecstasy, was, as with Zipp, administered orally. Effects were as rapid and long-lasting as those of Zipp, but involved predominantly the emotional responses of the target, rendering him prone to weeping at the least provocation, to extraordinary honesty in interactions with others, and to an openhandedness with his resources far in excess of what would be considered normal generosity.

Molly Liberation produced such gratifying results, in fact, that right up until the cataclysm of 1991, the League laboratory was concentrating all its efforts in the production of successor generations. One of these reportedly compelled the target multiple times a day to remove all his clothing and sing La Marseillaise; another promising iteration forced the target, when dining in a group, to impulsively grab food from the plates of others and consume it with his hands while making deep grunting noises.

So, onward. You're now in a position to better appreciate the events recounted in this sweet slice of journalism, events never before properly documented, covering the crucial period from 1987 to 1994. As much as these are part of League history, they also tell the tale of two of the most remarkable characters ever associated with the League: one a member, the other an outsider who pursued many of the League's goals as zealously as Dion himself. It is the story of their personal and professional struggles, their mysteriously entwined fates. The story of how, in pursuing justice as they saw it, they set themselves on a collision course with the hugely formidable foe, the vodka establishment, and in so doing forever transformed the world of wine and spirits. It is the story of Brewster Hotte and Margot Sipski.

Vinnie

Christchurch, NZ

September, 2006

NOTE ON DIALOGUE: In an age when authors are so often rightfully accused of fabricating material to suit their purposes, let me say without equivocation that all events in this book are true. However, because of a lack of source material, in many instances I have been forced to reconstruct dialogue for dramatic purposes. Let me stress that in each case I have done so only with the greatest care, keeping in mind the personality of the speaker, his or her history, and the specific situation. I have dealt with the issue of motivation and interior dialogue on that same basis. It is only in very rare instances that I have resorted to complete, shameless bullshit.

New York Daily Samsara — August 4, 1979

WINE AND SPIRITS WORLD RATTLED BY MYSTERY ATTACKERS

(Paris) In March of 1978, a high profile wine and spirits industry figure began a speech involuntarily quacking like a duck. In May of this year, a London banker with tens of millions of dollars in investment-quality French and Italian wines exhibited similar behavior. One month later, a nearly identical case was reported concerning a casino owner in New Jersey. Though far from being clear evidence of some dark global conspiracy, these incidents have sparked speculation about possible revenge attacks by disgruntled former employees with access to sophisticated pharmaceuticals, or perhaps some form of politically-motivated protest.

At this stage, law enforcement agencies investigating the incidents are primarily local, and are candid in admitting that they have little to go on. All have requested the involvement of national and international agencies, to bring greater resources to bear in shedding light on what might well be an operation of international scope.

Brett Boston, current chairman of the International Association for Alcohol Consumption, was quoted in a recent interview as saying there was no cause for panic. "There will always be crackpots on the fringes of society who want to disrupt the legal, honorable activities of making, selling, and consuming lots of alcohol. Will we ever catch all the health nuts, the neo-Prohibitionists, the wrong-headed activists who for whatever reason want to interfere with mankind's God-given right to do copious yet sensible drinking? Of course not. But we must do ourselves and the generations to come after us the honor of remaining steadfast in our commitment to potable ethanol. Just remember what Jesus said: 'What profiteth a partygoer if the spirits are willing but the drinks are weak?'"

Mr. Boston went on to offer some new recipes for refreshing summer drinks (see Home and Family section, p.3), after which he noted that if, out of fear, we decrease our alcohol production or consumption even slightly, it would not just be an overreaction, but a disgrace. "Once we do that, these ethanol terrorists win."

The San Francisco Times-Believer   December 5, 1984

SAN FRANCISCO SAYS FAREWELL TO NOTED BUSINESS AND POLITICAL LEADER

Erskine "Red" Hotte, three-term Congressman and founder of Spodie International Wine & Spirits, died yesterday of complications arising from liver and kidney failure. He was 67. He is survived by his wife of 35 years, Jane Dalraddy Hotte, and his two sons, Jackson (Jock) and Brewster, both of San Francisco.

Mr. Hotte founded his successful distribution company in 1950, following his discharge from the Naval Hospitality Corps where he served for five years as Chief Petty Mixologist for the Sixth Fleet. His elder son, Jackson, took the helm of the company in 1978, when Mr. Hotte was elected to the U.S. House of Representatives.

A universally beloved figure in the greater San Francisco Bay Area, "Red," as he was known to all, had a strong affinity for the common people. He often attributed his success to the support of "the little guy," the average drinker who showed such unwavering support for his flagship product, Isopropov Vodka.

During his tenure in Congress, he authored several sweeping pieces of legislation, most notable among them The Libation Assistance Act of 1980, more popularly known as the Drink Stamps Program. In the midst of floor debate on the measure, Mr. Hotte memorably said, "Make no mistake: To deny less fortunate Americans the right to relax, unwind, and knock back a few drinks every night is the very definition of discrimination."

Private memorial services will be held at Our Lady of the Happy Holy Hour in San Francisco, followed by a public celebration of his life at Crazy Feet Roller Rink in South City. Though the family has requested that it be a strictly BYOB event, everyone is encouraged to come down and, in a loud voice, tell your favorite stories about Red, put on some skates, and throw a few punches.

In lieu of flowers, contributions are being accepted by the Emergency Room Fund of San Francisco General Hospital.

AUGUST 28, 1991 BEFORE THE STORM

When it was all over, League members agreed that it was both absurd and ironic that the most momentous—and seemingly last—events in the history of the League should have involved no active members and have taken place in a scruffy, neglected parking lot near a freeway overpass in San Francisco, and in the sitting room of a sprawling, badly decorated Victorian. Most members had a high enough opinion of their work and sufficient imagination to locate such powerful events, whatever they might be, in a chic, or at least interesting, setting. Say, in the dining room of London's Hackford Chop House on the Strand, or in the shadows of a dim Bordeaux barrel *chai*, or in the chill northern light of a distilling chamber on the Isle of Skye.

The actual events were more like a marriage of film noir and James Bond, with a touch of keystone cops. They were completely foreseeable and an utter surprise.

The morning of August 28, 1991 was warm in the city, warm enough that Brewster ordered an iced cappuccino (extra chocolate) at The Caffiend before walking over to Margot's. Since she had catapulted to super-stardom, they were getting together more and more for business meetings with him in the role of her manager, rather than for wine tastings where he was always her devoted student.

He was hungover, yes, but on his personal scale of severity it was a Dean Martin, not a Richard Burton. And certainly not a Nick Nolte. On top of a headache and his usual melancholia, he was shouldering a larger than normal sack of woes, one that went beyond the irritation of still having Bernadette's yappy voice in his ear, years after the divorce, listing his many shortcomings in tweezer detail.

He was also crushed that after five years, Margot, the great fascination of his life, was no more interested in him sexually than, well, any other woman was. Physically, she was a pickup truck and not a sports car, it was true, yet her barge-like feet and hefty bones seemed perfectly balanced by her height, a lush head of ebony hair, her dramatic chin, and her generous eye makeup. She was great company—dry humor, folksy wit, fearless questioning—but far more committed to tasting and understanding wine and spirits than to any other project, including and especially men. He still couldn't accept it.

He was depressed, too, by his failures as a League operative. Though he'd had many celebrated successes—many more than his disasters—it was the botched assignments that he remembered best. And it was natural that his most recent, the so-called Chardonnaki operation that was launched the previous March, should sting the most. Despite efforts by myself and several other operatives, it had earned him a devastating year-long suspension from the League. It wasn't just the humiliation of it; it was the feeling of being *unmoored*, rudderless, up that famous creek without a paddle. It was depressing to face a life that was financially comfortable but without much traction, either in his own mind or in the world at large. He wrote his free-lance articles for magazines and newspapers, but without much relish. It was a way to pass the time until Margot agreed to get into his bed.

He walked the few blocks to her door, absently sipping his cappuccino. Margot buzzed him in using the security system Brewster had installed for her office and upstairs apartment after the pot-shot someone had taken at her window a couple of months before. It had left them both shaken, but the police called it a random act, unable to find any suspects or motives. Maybe a drunk blowing off steam, who could say for sure? Brewster didn't believe it for a second. Gunshots on 24th Street? Like unicorn sightings. Or discovering fine wines from Iceland. Margot might want to ignore the fact, but he knew she had made some real enemies.

That morning, as usual, they discussed her finances and upcoming appearances, each aware that the other was hiding something. They looked at each other, unable to be completely honest, thinking this was just another day and another conversation, another opportunity for throwaway teasing and the endless sparring they both seemed to enjoy.

"Those guys from Biggy Bob's Pork Fat Chips are still calling to get an endorsement deal. I told them to forget it," Brewster said.

"How much were they offerin'?"

"A lot. But it's just not your image."

Margot got exasperated. "Dammit if you're not walkin' on my toes again. You coulda asked me about it."

"Margot, my dear, those nitwits have just put out a *haggis*-flavored chip. Do you want to associate your good name with that? Do you?"

"You know, when I was poor as gully dirt, you could talk to me that way, but it's gettin' a little old. You can be such a stuck-up prig sometimes."

Brewster couldn't deny the charge.

BREWSTER

The all-purpose wine glass was an object of contempt for Brewster. "Why not an all-purpose golf club? Or how about an all-purpose gardening tool? An all-purpose sexual position?" he would say. I always loved to hear him "drink and drone," as he put it, voicing sweeping opinions at the League's semi-annual meetings held at the Control Hub. Though his observations were not always appreciated, he lived enough in the self-sufficiency lobe of his brain not to care much—to see himself, as he put it, as the love child of James Bond and Julia Child.

Which would have been accurate had he actually been a suave, rakish fellow and a good cook. As much as I revered him, I have to say: he was neither.

As it was, Brewster's rants were enough to damage his popularity in the League. He complained about everything from the salinity of the popcorn served at informal functions, to the quality of the mission targets selected by the League Steering Committee. It was especially galling for the Fourteen, the original members of the League, to accept this fussing and grousing, coming as it did from Number Fifteen, the first new member to be inducted into the League beyond the founding membership. Many felt it boded ill for their magnificent enterprise, but I was not among them.

I had lots of reasons to appreciate Brewster, not least because I felt he appreciated me. I freely admit that as a logistics operative I didn't have the sexiest job in the League, so I suppose it was normal that I should be less fussed-over than some members; but Brewster always had time for me, and not in that horrible, dismissive, pat-you-on-the-head way that I have sometimes encountered in my life. He didn't seem put off by my history of years spent sitting in an office moving Maersk ocean containers around the world, nor by the decade I spent being sure AT&T customer service employees had enough toilet paper, coffee, and recreational drugs to get through their shifts. He didn't care that my background was so solidly blue-collar, pointing out that most League members had similar roots, but were much more intent on hiding them.

The real proof of Brewster's friendship, however, lay in his tolerance of my foibles. How could I do anything but love a guy who came from considerable privilege but who didn't bat an eye when I told him about my attachment to the kinds of cooking my mother did in the late fifties, dishes straight out of the Betty Crocker and Better Homes and Gardens cookbooks? Not only did he maintain discreet silence about these potentially embarrassing revelations, but he indulged me. He often suggested, for instance, that when we were to meet for an OIE (Operation Information Exchange), as happened in preparation for most operations, the venue should not be some upscale café, but instead a place like one of the many Dippy's Diner locations, where I could get an extra-chewy fried chicken dinner, perfectly heat-lamp cured, or a plate of beef stew, with the zang of extra sodium in its rich, thick, corn-starch gravy, served with that magic mix of bouncy little carrot cubes and dimpled peas. There was never a hint of criticism in his manner—though I did note he most often ordered scrambled eggs for himself. He pointedly avoided ordering wine, while I happily enjoyed a glass of Chardonnay Rosé.

It is true that some members saw me as Brewster's lackey, but I reject that notion. Admiration and affection do not a toady make.

Brewster's selection for membership was due to the patronage of Dion, our League chairperson. Dion was a chemist by training, and an extraordinary one. He was also a monkish, stoop-shouldered, aging albino nerd, whose small, watery eyes and twitchy pink nose reminded one, ironically enough, of a lab rat. His pocket-protector appearance and mild manner gave no indication of his brilliant mind, however—a mind that had, amazingly, not been obliterated by the generous quantities of drugs he ingested in his youth. It was a mind that had not only conceived of the League, its mission, and its small but formidable arsenal of non-lethal weapons, but also had previously created several commercial products, the laser fingernail cutter and the From-Scratch Pizza Oven Lunchbox, the sale of the patents for which provided much of the capital required to fund the League and its activities around the world.

Oh, and as I mentioned already, he loved old pop music. Primarily songs from the sixties and seventies. This would have been nothing but an embarrassing quirk had he not decided early on that all League messages be encoded using a selection of these lyrics. There were loud complaints, initially, primarily about the ironic lack of taste such a move represented, but also about the difficulty of committing so much near-nonsense to memory. Several members mentioned the sheer indignity of it. Some operatives lobbied hard to adopt the code format used so successfully in the 1970s by the French DST (Directorate of Territorial Security), which utilized kitchen recipe instructions. They argued that picking up the phone and hearing a voice say "Working quickly, fold the egg whites into the broccoli puree" was infinitely preferable to hearing "Jam up and jelly tight; my, my, my, my baby now you're out of sight." But in the end the outcome was never in doubt, and all operatives became proficient in the use of largely inane song lyrics as code.

Brewster was elected to League membership in 1981, over energetic objections from some members. Why this spoiled trust fund baby, from a family of cheap vodka merchants? He should be a *target* of the League, not a member, they said. Rumor was that he was unstable, and drank too much. He was just a fringy freelance wine writer, anyway. How could he be a true Flavor Commando, a solid operative with the dedication and nerve to dose an enemy of good taste without exposing the League and everyone in it? But these objections were overruled by a majority led by Dion and Hideo, the latter an engineer by training, who derived his wealth from a hugely popular invention now in global use, the stethoscope warmer. He and Dion pointed out that Brewster's silver spoon background was precisely what the League needed to gain entry to exclusive gatherings where League targets most often surfaced in vulnerable circumstances. His connections, along with his cover as a legitimate freelance journalist, allowed him to operate in rarified circles, freely and without suspicion.

But the most powerful reason both Dion and Hideo insisted on Brewster's induction, and the source of much of my admiration for him, was the heartfelt and passionate quality of his writing. Oh, Brewster penned his share of mind-numbing puff pieces for *The Wine Stimulator* and *The National Intoxicator*, all right. Twenty-five hundred words of acreage statistics and glowing adjectives below photos of quirkily-dressed but attractive winemakers leaning on rows of barrels or standing in a vineyard examining the veins of a Chardonnay leaf like they were a treasure map. But just as often he wrote blunt, accurate assessments of the world of wine and spirits, insightful enough to piss off just about everyone in the industry. He also wrote the occasional searing satire. Though these appeared only in less mainstream publications like *Guzzler* and *The Binge*, they gave another dimension to Brewster's reputation, putting him in a class by himself as an industry journalist.

Such was the resistance to Brewster's membership in the League, however, that even after successfully completing four major operations, the grumbling continued. Heightened resentment could be traced to his promotion, in 1984, to Chief Operative for Super-Premium, Ultra-Premium, Extreme Premium, and Drop-Dead Premium products.

"Hotte is an asshole. An asshole who can barely tie his shoes. That's what." I heard that more than once from Impnitz, when I saw him in the main corridor of the Control Hub and made the mistake of casually asking what was going on. Impnitz, a former researcher at the National Institutes of Health, did pioneering work on the now-recognized health value of regular nasal applications of rum, and had published papers on the biochemistry of beer foam. But he was not an easy personality. He was short, jowly, and bald, except for a wispy gray fringe that hung to his shoulders. With crab-like little hands that were never still, he was all short-sleeve white shirts, Van Heusen suits, and wingtips. Knowing of my admiration for Brewster, he could be counted on to drop a sour comment about him, like spoor for me to step in, at times even unrelated to news of one of Brewster's triumphs.

Many times at conclaves, I gently reminded Brewster that Impnitz and some of the others were gunning for him, and that he should consider cutting a lower profile at meetings. He was always cavalier about it. He would say, "Does my being way up here on the flagpole make my butt look big?" Or "I consider it a fashion statement to have a target on my back." I had to love his brand of jovial, wry self-assurance, even if I suspected it was just part of his public face.

MEETING MARGOT, POLYESTER
NOTWITHSTANDING

And of course Brewster *could* be devastatingly effective in the field. True, he sometimes overindulged at the most unfavorable moments, but there was no better operative when he wasn't distracted by excellent food or—more often—by fine libations, especially those of the wine persuasion.

For instance, there was the difficult 1986 case of Jess McPecker, owner of a large winery and extensive vineyards in Northern California's Slobova and Foppo Counties. The League had documented the McPecker-financed development of prototypes for the Auto-Enologist, a computer/robotic winemaking system that aimed to eliminate flesh-and-blood winemakers. Yet bringing the fight to him was tough; he rarely made public appearances because of general paranoia and recent hair loss.

It was generally agreed that Brewster was the only choice for the assignment. Using his connections, he attended the annual preferred shareholders dinner and successfully slipped the target a six-year dose of ML, sprinkling the fine powder into two empty glasses at McPecker's place at the head table. In debriefing, Brewster said that the high visibility of the head table prevented him from using his hollow signet ring; instead he relied on his cuff link dispenser. In his usual tart fashion, he claimed that his only risk during the operation was possibly dying of boredom from drinking the faceless Chardonnay foisted on guests.

As I said, James Bond he was not. People often laughed at Brewster's appearance, yet it was his harmless, awkward look that allowed him to fly below enemy radar. He bitched about his waistline, his blood pressure, his straight sandy hair that flopped on his broad brow, his deathly pallor interrupted only by cheeks the color of carpaccio; still, he was adamant in declaring wine and food—French food, specifically—a huge and permanent part of his life. He often said he never wanted to know how much of his body weight was pure duck fat. He rarely ventured into the kitchen at all, and took virtually all his meals in higher-caliber restaurants and cafes, indulging his fondness for *foie gras* and excellent chocolate desserts, in particular. It was a habit that consumed a reckless portion of his inheritance. He described himself as a victim of his own experience, having prematurely concluded a chef's training course at the Cordon Bleu in Paris by starting a large, frightening grease fire which did substantial damage.

He favored Gucci loafers, triple-pleated pants, white monogrammed shirts, and bow ties. If he wore a jacket, it was most often linen, looking like he had wadded it up and stored it in his cheek for a few hours before donning it. Yet he was a consummate conversationalist, cultivated and strangely suave when motivated. He had an infectious, full-throated laugh, and if his voice was pitched a bit high, it had a soft, round tone which could be hypnotic.

Like so many momentous events, Brewster's historic

meeting with Margot Sipski, in March of 1987, was haphazard, and might even have been seen as comical had he not failed in his League mission that night. He had traveled to France's Burgundy region, where he was targeting the well-known wine producer, Didier Culotte, who had recently provided seed money to launch a new magazine, printed in English but targeting the international wine community, called *The Wine Screw.* The initial press release read in part: "What is more natural than wine? Sex, of course! We see our mission as exposing our readers to the vast possibilities in the synergistic relationship between wine and the sex act. It puts a bulge in the membrane of our winepress just thinking about the juicy pictorial features, the range of full-frontal historical, technical, and whimsical articles that celebrate the exciting and explicit connections between sipping and screwing!"

He was unanimously classified and targeted as a Prick.

The launch party was held at Culotte's ancient cellars in Beaune, and drew a crowd of about three hundred people. Following his failed mission, at the debriefing back at the Control Hub, Brewster was very candid about what transpired.

"I was waylaid, waylaid by—well, not actually, you know, not *laid*, as such, no. I was entranced, let's say, by the wines at some of the tasting stations set up around the cellar. I hadn't expected to see truly great Burgundies! So when I saw the '53 Richebourg from Jean Creepeau, and the '59 Bonnes Mares from Albert Fécale, I felt obliged to pitch in with the work of consuming them."

Which is how, about an hour later, when his target, Culotte, had already left the party, Brewster said he suddenly found himself lying on the cellar floor, momentarily befuddled. And it was at that moment that Margot Sipski stepped on his hand.

"I'll never forget the thrill of pure pain that shot up my arm, just as I will never forget seeing her for the first time," he told me, a few years later. "I howled loudly, of course, and sat up to assess the situation. There was a woman, kneeling. I saw first a rather spectacular décolletage, strained to capacity, tilted solicitously toward me. There was glowing, rosy skin and a long, liquid neck that focused my attention wonderfully. She wore a cheap-looking periwinkle cocktail dress—polyester blend—but I barely registered it. In the confusion, seeing her rich ebony hair falling on her shoulders, and the thick stripes of eyeliner framing her caramel-colored eyes made me wonder: Is she Egyptian? An Egyptian cocktail waitress, perhaps?"

Brewster went on to say that she appeared more annoyed than apologetic. He wondered dazedly whether she would let him maul her if he were pathetic enough. Their first exchange was this:

Margot: *Qu'est-ce que tu fous là, par terre?* (Translation note: This is a vulgar way of asking, What are you doing on the ground? Brewster noticed her excellent accent—better than his. He was unsure of her nationality at this point.)

Brewster: *J'étais fatigué.*

Margot: You're a damn American!

Brewster: So are you, by the sound of it. Are you planning to walk on me a little more, or will you help me up? You could join me down here, if you like.

Brewster reported that she did not laugh, or even smile.

HUNG OVER, IN LOVE

Once on his feet, he noticed Margot's height. Two or three inches taller that he, probably six feet. And muscular, with an extra helping of hips. She guided him over to a row of chairs along a wall close to the cellar entrance. Through the noise of the shifting crowd, the fog of alcohol, the haze of anxiety about missing Culotte and aborting his assignment, he was amazed to feel so much—what?— animal energy surrounding her like a nimbus. It made him want to keep her there, next to him. Maybe try to maul her when his motor skills returned. But for the moment remorse was dominant.

"I hate myself," he moaned, head tilted back, eyes closed.

"Seems a little harsh, if you ask me. I never like to jump right on the prosecution's bandwagon before I hear from the defense team."

"My guy escaped!" he said.

Margot regarded him with the barest hint of a smile. "Well, it's pretty much true your fly's open, I'll give you that. But there's no sign of a jailbreak. Unless you meant somethin' else."

He slowly brought his dazed eyes down to meet hers, then struggled briefly with his zipper. "Terrible way...

learn…humility. Why not? Sorry," he mumbled. "Must have lost my footing back there." He shot her a ghastly smile, with drooping eyelids. "The real question is, have you tasted the extraordinary wines…down the way… there?" He gestured lamely back toward the spot where he had fallen.

She pursed her lips. "Nope. Just a few of the ones over near the food table. I was stopped by a drunk guy lyin' on the floor."

He sputtered a laugh. "Very good, good. Thanks again. For helping."

"You mean thanks again for walkin' on my hand with your size tens?"

He couldn't help looking down at her black, open-toe, low heels. Even in his stupor he could see: they *were* large. "Why don't we…let's call it a rescue. I'll buy you dinner sometime. Compensation."

She fixed him with a frank, open stare. "I'm pretty busy. Lots of wines to taste in Burgundy. Why don't you tell me your name, how about that?"

"Very fair request. I'm Brewster Hotte, H-O-T-T-E. The opposite of cold. Freelance writer, from San Francisco."

She lit up. "Damn, what a great city, practically my home turf! I used to visit when I was workin' at the Pudworth Estate, up in Slobova County, right after I graduated from Fresno State."

"So how did you end up here?"

"A nice girl like me in a place like this, you mean? Well, I'm not here for an advance copy of the dumb-ass magazine, for sure. I heard from my boss that they were gonna have great wines at this shindig. So here I am."

"Who's your boss, if you don't mind my asking?"

"I was lucky as hell. Right place at the right time. I'm doin' a *stage* 'til August up in Gevrey, with Andre Ruineux."

"Ruineux!" His eyes widened in spite of his stupor. "Well *that's* impressive. Lucky you."

"I'm learnin' a lot, and I actually like the cellar work. When I've got time to myself I tool around in a truck they let me use so I can taste at other domains. Pretty damn interestin'."

"I still don't know your name."

"It's Margot. Margot Sipski. From Fresno." She held out her hand and gave Brewster a firm grip and three quick shakes. He could sense her restlessness. "Well, Mister Hotte..."

He gripped her forearm gently. She wouldn't get away if he could help it. "Listen, I know these caterers, so why don't you let me forage for a little nourishment? With something interesting to drink, what do you say?"

"You think you can walk? And carry stuff too?"

He gave her a wry look as he stood up. Wobbly at first, but with an ironclad desire to impress Margot, he walked down one tunnel-like wing of the cellar where he had seen the caterers working. He brought back a small plate of *gougères* and Gruyère tartlettes along with a couple of glasses of '79 Meursault Charmes from Jean Locaux.

"Whatcha got?" Margot asked.

"Just taste and enjoy. The luxury of being in Burgundy, where some of the most expensive headaches in the world are born. Like mine, for instance."

This was the moment when Margot thrilled him as surely as if she had let him maul her. She swirled the wine in her glass, pinching the stem oh so delicately between a meaty thumb and index finger, then carefully tasted—and *named* it. The producer, the vineyard and the vintage. Bang. Just like that.

He was sure she had cheated somehow. Though there were easily forty wines available from the various tasting stations at that gathering, she must have memorized them all. Or…something.

She gave him a reproving look. "So I'm wrong, is that it?"

He assured her that she was right and that he was stone-cold impressed. His mind was seething and he spoke without thinking. "Not to insult you or any such thing, but would you mind if I brought you a couple of other wines to—try?"

"You mean you wanna treat me like some kinda damn trained seal? How could I be insulted by that?"

"No, no, oh God, that's not what I meant. I was only—"

"Oh yeah it was. That's just what you meant." She sighed. "But I don't mind so much. Same kinda thing happened last winter in Chablis."

He brought her another white and a red, both of which she identified exactly. He forgot about his headache, and dug deep to locate a reservoir of extra charm. This woman wasn't just attractive: she was a genius. He would have to get her some new clothes, but her talent could be a huge boost to Spodie International if Jock and his mother ever allowed him a say in things. Or maybe even a big addition to the League, who could tell? Dizzy and still reasonably drunk, it was impossible for him to separate his lust from his amazement and professional admiration. Though smiling was never one of his strongest skills—he'd been told that when he makes the attempt he looks like someone in serious pain—he gave it his best effort. It was no help that in his mind he could hear his ex-wife Bernadette's description of him as a bad combination of aloof and needy.

"Margot, I'm sure you've thought of this, but with your skills you could do wine education classes, demonstrations, put out a newsletter. So many options."

"Make some bucks, right? Be a circus sideshow. Look, first of all I love makin' wine, and I'm still learnin' about that. After I'm done at Ruineux, I'm lookin' to get more internships in other parts of France, if I can. Sancerre, the western Loire, Cote Rotie, Alsace. There's a whole lot I don't know. And just because I can stick my snotwand into a glass and tell you about the wine doesn't mean I'm done learnin'. I'm not goin' home 'til I've crammed as much as I can into my little pea brain."

"But you could still—"

"Listen, I've seen enough of the wine business to know what I *don't* want, and that's to be corralled into some glitzy punk-ass project that's all flash and no flavor. I'm in it for the taste, period. I'm obsessed and crazy and all that stuff, and I figure that'll be my north star for quite a long while."

They talked for more than an hour, Brewster fighting with his sodden brain to keep Margot interested. He was incredulous that he could be so powerfully drawn to any woman, but especially this woman: campy clothes, large bones, eyeliner and all. Its causes might be obscure, but the attraction itself certainly wasn't.

"Margot Sipski, you absolutely have to make some time to have dinner with me before I leave on Friday. I'll bet you haven't had the *coq au vin* at La Lécheur. Classic."

She looked dismissive. "I tried it, yeah. It's okay. Not as good as you get at Le Canard Sans Foie in Dijon, though."

"Seriously? You've eaten at both of those restaurants, and you prefer the Canard Sans Foie? Never been there—I keep telling myself I've got to try it. But I can't believe theirs is better than La Lécheur's. They use really nice wine in that sauce, I can tell you."

She smiled. "So we're having a pissin' contest! My favorite. But the difference between the two is big time. There's lots of differences, really, but the biggest one is that La Lécheur thickens their sauce with butter and flour. The Canard thickens theirs with chicken blood; they mix it with the ground liver and good local *marc*." She eyed him meaningfully. "It's got five times the flavor. Super rich."

Brewster's tidy side rose up and spread a grimace on his face. "Is something like that okay with the health inspectors? Sounds pretty…earthy."

"You're not one of those sanitized, white bread gourmets, are you?"

"I didn't think I was." Brewster saw an opening here, and paused for effect. "But okay, then. If I am, you've got a clear duty now, ma'am. You have *got* to let me take you up to Dijon, for my first visit. My first look at their *coq au vin,* come on." Amazingly, she agreed.

"So now you know how I spend my time—and money," she said.

Brewster's unkind thought: "You're certainly not spending it on clothes." But he said nothing. He'd been drinking, yes, but he wasn't completely self-destructive.

When they finally noticed that the crowd had thinned

and the catering staff was collecting plates and abandoned glasses, they stood to leave. Brewster was still just drunk enough to ask her if she was romantically involved with anyone.

"I am, yeah. With wine. Like I told you. It's a long-term relationship." She gave him the lopsided wry smile he would eventually come to know well. "You really don't like my dress, do you?"

THE STALK-A-THON

After a long, lingering dinner the next night, most of which Brewster spent feeling privately humiliated by Margot's deep knowledge of French cuisine and wine, he found himself disastrously in love. He could hardly focus on his bungled League mission the night before, much less on looming deadlines for writing assignments. She was wry and funny, self-deprecating but whip smart. Worst of all for Brewster, she looked more and more beautiful. His fantasies were consuming him: not just getting his mouth all over her generous body, but also getting a Pygmalion-like shot at her wardrobe, her manner—maybe even her makeup. Why was this happening? Didn't he worship her just as she was? Why the crying need to manipulate her? Until Margot picked him up off the floor, his only serious reference for so-called feelings of love was his relationship with Bernadette, his ex-. And in that relationship, *he* had been Eliza Doolittle. She wanted a more genial, less angst-ridden version of Brewster, someone with well-oiled social graces as well as piles of money. Someone who would be a genuine asset in her efforts to scale the heights of success in her chosen field, which was catering. "Brewster, why don't you just relax at cocktail parties? Maybe wear a sporty-looking tie. You're there to have fun! To talk with interesting people! Sweetie, please just try, okee? For me. You are so much more handsome when you smile!" She shook her little head and fluttered her lashes; he found it all so sweet and charming.

At first.

He told himself he had to rein in his makeover urges for Margot. He knew what it felt like to be on the receiving end of that mania. It would never pay off.

The debriefing back at the Control Hub was painful, but Brewster knew the territory. He sat at the small conference table, sheepish, nursing his bottle of Badoix water, fantasizing about Margot. Across from him were Dion and the two senior operatives who had just rotated into their year of debriefing duties. There was a tape recorder in the middle of the table, recording the proceedings. He tried to be upbeat. Fine, he had botched it, okay, but this woman was a find! A great addition to the community of real wine and spirits lovers. Maybe even a League member one day.

Dion and the others were expressionless. "This was the woman who tripped over your body. On the floor of the cave," said Dion.

"But they were pouring Creepeau's '53 Richebourg! I'm only flesh and blood." Painful silence. "And after all, it's very possible my drunken klutz routine is actually the best cover I could have!"

Brewster received a formal reprimand, but his star rose again a few months later, when he successfully dosed the chairman of Vomette Frères, S.A., a French wine producer who had traveled to Virginia to negotiate a possible collaboration with R. J. Ribaldus Tobacco Company. The new product was to be called "Chawdonnay," and was touted as a revolution in smokeless tobacco. Freeze-dried alcohol, so long a chimera in chemistry, had finally been harnessed to produce a supposedly perfect blend with tobacco. "Just a pinch between gum and lip, and you're set for hours of great flavor and a righteous buzz!" Brewster was cited by the League for creativity in impersonating an employee of the club where the chairman golfed the day before the meeting. He administered an eight-to-nine-year dose of Molly Liberation I to the water bottles of the entire foursome, reportedly including several Ribaldus officials. Praised for years afterward, it was flawless use of his League-issued single-bottle closure unit (designed to handle glass and plastic bottles, corks or screwcaps) that allowed him to create dosed bottles indistinguishable from factory-sealed ones. At the press conference later that day, the Vomette chairman sobbed bitterly at intervals, revealing that he had conspired with Ribaldus to cut the product ingredients with pulverized drywall scraps from large construction sites. He also confessed that the woman who had handled much of the Ribaldus legal work on the deal was insatiable in bed.

Meanwhile his obsessing about Margot had created a plan: long-term, big picture stalking. Wherever she was in France, he would find her. Share a meal, a glass of wine, or—even better—a chocolate dessert. Get in her good graces if possible, but if not, at least get in her face. He remembered she said she would next be going to Alsace to work the crush at the Butschling estate near Colmar, so he arranged an 'accidental' meeting at a nearby restaurant she frequented. Fancy that! You, here! We've got to stop meeting like this!

Over the next three years, he met her 'by chance' in Reims, in Tours, in Bandol, in Auxerre, in Avignon. He even engineered a meeting with her in Paris, where in early 1989 she had gone to visit a French friend, Juliénas Morgon, who had graduated with her from Fresno State. He eased into the brasserie banquette next to her, grinning broadly as he signaled the waiter for another wine glass. This is really crazy, isn't it? *Complètement dingue*!

Each meeting made him more excited, but more depressed, too. It was thrilling to bathe in her aura, to take in the graceful blades of onyx hair falling around the strong features of that face; but it was depressing to have her continue to parry all his offers of a drink up in his hotel room, or even a nice walk in some possibly romantic venue. It was frustrating, but Brewster was not the type to give up.

Things finally changed in June of 1990, when he engineered another, more extended meeting. The occasion was one of many glam-fests held by various chateaux in the Bordeaux region of France during the huge, week-long trade show called VinRex, a popular combination of orgy and workaholism that attracts tens of thousands of those partial, if not to wine itself, then at least to alcohol. Or, at a minimum, to money. These invitation-only dinners were intended to bring order to the scrum of sweaty social climbers who vied for position in the world of wine clout. To receive an invitation from one of the elite, first-tier chateaux, well, that signaled near-royalty. To attend any events at all was to be positioned as one of the elect. And with his connections, Brewster was often enough among them.

It goes without saying that I myself never attended

VinRex. I'm the one with his nose pressed up against the figurative windowpane.

This particular dinner was held at Chateau Mouche-Tapette, a well-regarded, solidly second-tier producer in the township of St. Julien. The dinner was a hot ticket because the wines of the chateau had improved by leaps and bounds in recent years. The new owner—an insurance company—had sunk loads of money into re-planting vineyards and buying new equipment, and naturally the wine community wanted to bask in the glow.

Just after arriving, sweating heavily in blue oxford shirt, pink bowtie, and an ecru linen jacket that looked like elaborate, recently-unfolded origami, he had secured a glass of the chateau's indifferent Sauvignon Blanc and had positioned himself near the front entry, where he knew there would always be a server with a tray of *canapés* to sustain him. Because he wasn't on assignment for the League that evening but was contracted to write a feature article for *The Trough and Barrel*, a wine and food magazine, he could afford to feel relaxed and avuncular while waiting for Margot's arrival. It was as if he were standing at a window, watching children play in the back yard. Wine luminaries from various countries arrived, pausing on the gritty flagstones of the entry hall for a *Wine Stimulator* magazine photo. When a server finally pried his hand off the rim of a tray of especially delicious smoked sturgeon toasts, he turned back to the scene at the entrance, which was when he saw Margot.

A surge of adrenalin jolted him. Even then he couldn't help but be a bit critical of her hair, swept up carelessly in back. She was wearing a three-quarter length aqua skirt and the most unflattering baggy white cotton tunic, which featured bright red "peasant" embroidery. Unfortunate.

She seemed frustrated, bent over the reception table just inside the door, talking earnestly with two hostesses. It was obvious she was being turned away.

It didn't take Brewster more than a moment to identify an opportunity even juicier than the one he had envisioned. He stepped over to the table and put his right hand gently on Margot's back, giving the hostesses his most relaxed smile along with his maximum-bonhomie voice. "Is there an issue here?" And: "Ah, well, it's all perfectly explainable, Mesdames. She is with me!" Moments later the two of them were standing in the crowded reception hall— think Harry Potter's Hogwarts—drinking uninteresting Sauvignon Blanc.

Between sips, she gushed her thanks. "You're one generous guy, that's for sure. I owe ya bigtime." she said, placing a hand gently on his forearm.

He held her glance, sure that his heart would stop. He shrugged slightly and smiled. "We'll have to talk about how to structure that debt, huh?"

She was the first to look away. "At least this stuff is cold," she said, frowning at her glass. It was the first time he had seen her clearly flustered: beautifully flushed cheeks, abashed manner. Those wonderful milk chocolate eyes, and that energy. Whatever it was.

"I don't know what happened, I swear! The Butschlings said the invitation was all set!"

Brewster stiffened. "The Butschlings?" Those guys again. A father and son producer of decent but hopelessly overpriced Alsatian wines. They had terrible taste in music, too. During his most recent visit in the course of chasing Margot, the speakers in their offices and reception area were all Bee Gees and Lionel Richie. Not really grounds for League targeting, but putting them on his own personal watch list. The son, Fabrice, was particularly irritating, with his sculpted-jaw good looks, shoulder-length hair, narrow waist, and thirst for publicity. Or was this just Brewster's personal problem?

"Right! They've been the best kind of terrific to me. They seemed to like my work enough to give me an invite to work another crush at the estate. I'm pretty pumped up. Givin' it some serious thought."

How insane that he should feel a great stab of possessiveness toward this person he hardly knew. Yet when the hilt of the jealousy knife is sticking out of your chest and the floor is thick with blood, it is useless to deny it. "That's wonderful. I mean, as far as it goes…"

"What d'you mean?"

What did he mean? What did he *mean*? She had to be joking. She was going to go off to this obscure little estate in Alsace *again*, and waste—what?—three months or more, learning to handle odd-ball grape varieties like *Gewurztraminer,* for God's sake? She who could be educating, lecturing, displaying her tasting talent to a thirsty public had decided instead to go off into the wilderness and make Pinot Fucking Gris. And probably end up fucking Fabrice, too, if she hadn't already. It was more than he could bear. Luckily, his irritation found distraction when a server passed by with a tray. "Oh," he said, far too loudly, "you must try a few of these smoked sturgeon toasts, they're fantastic. Here," he said, passing her a cocktail napkin with four toasts balanced on it.

"You're gonna have to eat a couple of these," she said, juggling the napkin and her wine glass. "I'm savin' myself for the main event."

He plucked a toast from her napkin. "I love a challenge," he said, his mouth already full.

When the crowd was called to dinner, they crossed the gravel courtyard—Margot leaning heavily on him, unsteady even on modest heels—and entered one of the old *chais* that had been refurbished as a banquet hall. Four huge wrought iron chandeliers with vine and leaf motifs lit the space with warm coppery light, reflected in rows of gleaming stemware on crisp table linen. Place cards bearing each guest's name had been set out on the dozen large round tables; Brewster was unabashed as he cajoled a seventy-ish woman wearing a tiara to vacate her spot so that he might sit next to Margot. He beamed as he returned from escorting the woman to another seat.

Margot rolled her eyes. "God, but you really are the middle fork of Bullshit River."

The meal was like heaven for him, though it had nothing to do with the food or wine. Minus the terrible tension of a League assignment, he could enjoy making Margot laugh, and be completely content facing a composed salad of shriveled, leathery smoked duck and an incinerated rack of lamb, accompanied by remarkably dull old vintages of Mouche-Tapette. Recounting all this to me a month later, he joked that he would rather have faced some of my coffee shop fried chicken than wade through the fare that night.

"I really want to apologize again for my bad behavior

at that terrible reception in Beaune. It was inexcusable," he told her.

"How about we call it 'gone'? I didn't love the whole idea of that scuzzy magazine, and on top of it I had to wear girl clothes to get in the place, so I'm not exactly cherishin' the memory, anyhow."

Brewster confessed that it was his weakness for great old hard-to-find wines that brought him there, and triggered his shameless guzzling. "The worst is, I'm a predictable recidivist, if the wine is good enough. You know, it's kind of 'stop me before I kill again' stuff."

She offered her faint smile. "Well, we're both sittin' in amen corner on that one. But for me, it's just 'til I get the warm glow, you know—I don't do the fallin' down part."

They talked about music (Beethoven for him, Johnny Cash and Chopin for her). She didn't share his enthusiasm for Paul Simon. "The guy's a depressive," she insisted. They talked about the disaster at Chernobyl, Brewster wondering out loud if Burgundies were going to glow in the dark for a while if the prevailing winds were unfavorable.

"It'd be the same for the poor Butschlings in Alsace, too, if that's true," she said.

"Mmmm. Yes. Right," he said, trying to sound concerned.

Brewster confessed years later that all through that evening he was being turned upside down by the peculiar power of her, some animist elixir in her veins that seeped out and hovered all around, like the exotic atmosphere of her personal body-planet.

THE VODKA TANTRUM

After Brewster's sensibilities had been bruised by a sickly sweet slice of *reine de saba*, made with clearly substandard chocolate, and as coffee was being poured, a short, graceful man with delicate features, olive complexion, and a dark helmet of slicked-back hair appeared at Brewster's elbow. "Monsieur Hotte? I am Gontron Excisse, *régisseur* here at Chateau Mouche Tapette. I am pleased to meet you! I understand you are writing a piece about us for *Trough and Barrel*?" Impeccably dressed in an Italian suit, with the subtlest soap smell—maybe lemon verbena—surrounding him, he invited Brewster for some "further refreshment" in the salon of the main house. And of course his friend was welcome as well.

Margot was hesitant until Brewster assured her that there would be interesting Cognacs, Armagnacs, and *digestifs* to try.

What neither of them had counted on was the vodka.

As they sat with perhaps a dozen others in the busily ornate room, with its Louis XV chairs, its baby grand piano, its azure walls and eggshell trim with gilt accents, waiters in garish livery and white gloves circulated with carts carrying a menagerie of exotic bottles.

A pudgy older server with neatly parted gray hair

regarded them with kindly eyes. "What may I offer you this evening? Perhaps a Laberdolive Armagnac from 1959? Or a Louis XIII Cognac? A superb Calvados? In addition, we also have whiskeys, of course; and the Blottoskaya Apex Vodka."

Brewster had not yet witnessed a full display of Margot's wrath, so he was caught unawares. He sat in stunned silence as she sputtered at the waiter, jumping back and forth between French and English. "What the hell's a vodka doing here? *Cette merde, avec ces belles eaux de vie? Franchement, vous plaisantez?* I've got half a mind to dump that bottle out in front of the building right now—but I'm afraid I'd kill the landscaping! There's no excuse for this!"

When she finally paused to take a breath, the room was deathly silent, all eyes on them. Brewster took her by the arm, saying "Shall we take a walk?"

The server smiled weakly. "*Bonne soirée, Monsieur-Dame.*"

Once outside in the balmy, moist night air, she calmed down. He offered to drive her back to Bordeaux in his rental car, since she had taken a special shuttle bus from downtown Bordeaux to the event. In the car, he looked sidelong at her, wonderingly, as she explained her views on vodka. He had never heard her speak at such length, nor so passionately.

"Vodka's a joke. *C'est nul!* Who drinks the shit, anyway? People who do shots, people looking for the most efficient drunk. It's one step from frat boys slammin' beers. I'm not sayin' people shouldn't be free to drink as much of the stuff as they like. It's fine with me. Fine as frog's hair.

But nobody should expect to list it with the great drinks of the world. That's just bogus."

"I'm not unsympathetic, Margot." All the while, of course, Brewster was sweating, thinking about Spodie International and the Isopropov label. The one that built the family fortune. Could he tell her? When? Trying to sound objective, he continued. "Still, you've got to admit there are some vodkas that are well-positioned, profitable high-end products. Like Insolent, the one from Sweden. Or Splatnikov, the American one; they've got some new super-premium label now, called Diamond, I think. It shows that—"

"It shows there's one born every minute. Look, I don't care if the stuff is made from winter wheat, or from rye or potatoes or goddam chia seeds blessed by the Dalai Lama. It's still just a bunch of clear alcohol that's been distilled three or four times to be sure there's no character left in the stuff. And then they'll tell you the water they use is purer than anybody else's, or that they filter it through charcoal or platinum or a giraffe anus; but it's never really about taste, never about flavor—unless they dump coriander or some shit in it. At best, you're talkin' about texture! What a crock." She put her head back and came out with a single "Ha!" "And you oughta be in my corner, Brewster. You came to Bordeaux to go to VinRex, you taste a lot of wine. You're a really smart guy! You know about flavor."

He parked in the garage of his hotel, L'Aquitaine, on the Cours de l'Intendance. The air was close, and he could feel his nerves chattering, the sheen of sweat on his forehead, beads on his upper lip. He watched her stretch like a big cat when she got out of the car, all legs and rib cage and breasts. He was almost relieved when she refused to come up to his room for a mini-bar drink ("Like you don't know they stock those things with junk like Insolent vodka.")

"You know I'm not trying to hustle you, right? I'm not some *dragueur*." Why did he feel so off balance?

"I get that, I do," she said. "If I thought you were just some guy tryin' to get his turtle in the mud, I'd have been long gone by now. Trust me."

She agreed to let him walk her up the Rue Sainte Catherine, past the Palais du Sport, to her hotel on the other side of the old town.

As they walked, he rested his arm lightly around her waist. He was positively giddy when she made no move to escape. He was nervous in the silence, so he made jittery conversation, telling her about some of his interviews with various California winemakers—drunk ones, bitter ones, macho ones. She told him about applying for internships in Champagne, being chased around the room by old *roués* with pencil mustaches, wearing foulards. Their steps echoed faintly on the sidewalk as they walked through pools of amber light, the salty tang of the estuary in the warm air.

"I got a question for you," she said, looking sidelong at him.

"I've got a question for *you*, too. Do you believe in love at first sight?"

"No. But I believe in love at first taste. And the few years I've spent over here've made me a real wine floozy."

"But you're some kind of wine nun! What about love, intimacy? What about sex?"

She shook her head. "Wine is way better than sex."

46

"Not possible. I'd say you just haven't found the right partner."

"I'd say you just haven't found the right wines. But let me ask a question about you."

Brewster laughed, a little relieved to escape the drift of the conversation. "Sure. I just love talking about myself, anyone will tell you that."

"Cut it out. Stop posturing. I hate posturing."

"You hate posturing and you chose to work in the wine world?"

"Okay, okay. *Touché*. My burden to bear. But here's the question: you're a guy with some resources, that's for sure. Your weird clothes—no offense—your manners, every-thing screams it. And you wouldn't know so much about rare wine, and have tasted so much of it if you weren't pretty flush. So if you're so out-of-control in love with great wines, why don't you just buy a truckload of 'em, lock yourself in a room and drink yourself into the land of harps and halos?"

Margot had touched a nerve. The truth was, in the years after his breakup with Bernadette—until he met Margot at least—Brewster's work with the League was the only thing that kept him focused, but he clearly couldn't say that. Betraying his oath of silence about the League was out of the question, and telling her how attracted he was to her would risk scaring her away. So he used a convenient excuse.

"I can't find the great wines anymore! Not the ones from terrific vintages, with bottle age. No one wants to sell the real greats. But then it's probably a blessing. I'd just drink myself to death, as you say. You know, back when

I was a morose display of acne, my father got into one of his big rages—vodka-fueled, which you would certainly appreciate—screaming about how he hated mum's wine collection. So he sold it. The whole thing; and there were a lot of great old wines in there. Mum and I were heartbroken, and I'm sure my brother would have been, if his factory equipment had included either a heart or a palate. He's only interested in rape and merger." He registered her look of confusion and gestured dismissively. "It's a whole saga. But I can see now I'm better off without all those great bottles. Too much temptation."

Margot seemed satisfied with that. At the door of the hotel, they stopped and faced each other. "Thanks for an excitin' evening," she said, smiling. "Or maybe I should say, 'sorry for the excitin' evening.'"

"No, no, not at all! It was great. The excitement was, uh, all mine." He smiled as widely as he could, hoping to dispel his nervousness. He leaned in to kiss her, but she was too quick for him, turning her head so his lips met her cheekbone. She smiled and rolled her eyes as she made her way inside.

Brewster told me many times how at that moment he felt like a 15-year-old. A nerd. But on the other hand, it hadn't been a wasted evening. First of all, he had seen her again, and she seemed to be warming to him. He had come to her rescue at the door! He even remembered to give her his business card, and she promised to visit when she came back to California. But how long would he have to wait for *that*?

FROM THE BREWSTER ARCHIVE: BACKWASH MAGAZINE — MARCH 1987

Wine Drinkers: If you're reading this, you're probably a snob. I know I am. But at least I'm not a hypocrite, not someone who gets all bubbly about fine wine as the birthright of all God's children. Someone who spews all the hokum about the "golden age of wine" we are currently enjoying, where everyone has access to the riches of the wine world. I'm not a hypocrite because I'm willing to tell you the truth: There is a sign above the entrance to the world of fine wine, and that sign reads, "Wealthy Patrons Only."

And of course it's true. Anyone can plunk down eight dollars and buy something labelled "Chardonnay," but it's only fine wine in your dreams. It's actually a cunningly manipulated, trafficked, down-and-dirty concoction that uses every possible technical trick to hide the fact that it is a faceless mass of cheap crap. It's the pig with lipstick, the spray-on tan. It's "gourmet" French fries. It's bad costume jewelry.

Don't get me wrong: much of the stuff is potable. It's wet, alcoholic, and usually sugary enough to slide down the average throat without triggering the gag reflex. With some foods, it's better than beer. If you drink a couple of scotches beforehand, you can even anesthetize yourself into believing some of them are good. An overworked and/ or underqualified wine critic might be willing to award them 9000 points or a drawerful of gold medals from the Oklahoma State Pie-Eating Contest and Wine Competition. Yet nothing will get any of this swill past the velvet ropes that define "fine wine." To a real wine lover, it will never be much more appealing than a careless rectal examination.

By contrast, fine wine has character. It is from a particular place, with unique soil and climate, elements that give it a personality. And it has history. The excellence of any fine wine is not acknowledged after ten or twenty years. It is a consensus of knowledgeable experts over many decades, or even centuries. Fine wine is most often produced by people fiercely dedicated to the product and its heritage, as opposed to those who are fiercely dedicated to turning a profit or dominating the glitz media, however temporarily. Fine wine is less than 10 percent of all of the world's wine, and its rarity and pricing are what fuel the legendary snobbism of those who own and consume it. And read about it. Don't kid yourself: even if you're just spending a stupidly high percentage of your income on pricey wine, that snob is you.

MUM JANE, CORDIALLY

Two days back from France, Brewster was spending the morning in his two-story office flat, one of five almost identical units on 24th Street given to him by his parents when he turned twenty-one. He had moved in two years ago, when Bernadette had gone banshee on him. Three years of marriage to Brewster was apparently all she could manage. "Benign neglect does *not* cut it!" she had screeched at him. He was very open in admitting to the accuracy of her list of complaints. He was always pre-occupied. Couldn't seem to listen to her. Slashed her clothing budget. Had no friends of his own and hated hers. Away from home a lot, while not making much of a name for himself in journalism. That last one was the most damning item for Bernadette: lack of ambition.

He was relieved to leave her with the hulking painted lady of a Victorian in Pacific Heights. Living in the modest apartment upstairs from his office suited him very well.

As offices go his was a spacious one, with large bay windows giving onto the street, leather sofa and chair in one corner, a small wet bar, a refrigerator, and a 240-bottle wine cooler in another. On the walls, framed classic posters advertising Valrhona and Canzenave chocolate, along with an enlargement of the 1959 Chateau Mouton Rothschild label. The space smelled of popcorn and stale wine.

Still jet-lagged, he sat at his great aircraft carrier of a walnut desk, reclining in his chair, feet up. He had just begun Chapter Twelve of Don DeLillo's *White Noise* when the phone rang. He held the book open with one hand while he answered.

"This is Brewster."

He heard electronic distortion, an echo, a scramble of glissando-lush strings, guitar, and the crooning of a vocalist. A foreground voice battled with the noise. "Nipper? I'm including you for dinner tomorrow. Jock and Carolyn will be here—"

"What? Is that you, Mum? I can't—Is that Johnny *Mathis*? Could you turn it down, please? Or off? Better still. Yes, great. Thank you."

"Did you hear what I said? You're included for dinner tomorrow, with Jock and Carolyn. We have some business matters to discuss. At seven."

"Well. It's nice to hear from you."

"Now don't get smart with me. I'm counting on you to be here."

"But I'm otherwise engaged."

"Why do you have to be such a pill, Nipper? Whatever it is, you can reschedule. Corinne is making coulibiac of salmon and that lovely orange Bavarian cream for dessert—the one Bernadette used to make. You can't disappoint us on this."

"I can at least try, though, can't I? Especially my big brother —who is, parenthetically, a capacious sack of shit."

"Oh dear God. Please stop it." He could hear her taking a deep drag on her Benson & Hedges 100. "You've always been such a vulgar boy, just like your father."

"It's all about tradition. But Mum? If I'm going to show up, there are a couple of things I need from you."

"Please keep it reasonable."

"Always. One, I need some idea of the agenda. And two, I need to know if I will at any time actually be required to speak."

"Oh, for God's sake. Honestly. You will be expected to carry on a conversation with other members of your family, yes. How burdensome for you. And I don't know exactly what we'll be talking about. Some ideas for the future of the company. Whatever. It's up to Jock. I want to talk about getting a wine cellar back in the house here, too. Such a shame Bernadette isn't in the picture anymore, to see it happen. What a sensible girl, with such good taste, too."

"Perfect. You can invite her, and let me off the hook."

"Nipper, I'm just making an observation. You are always so touchy. If only you—"

"Touchy about a divorce. Imagine." He concentrated on relaxing his jaw. "It's good news about the wine cellar, though, I'll say that. You must be excited."

"I really am. It's been almost three years since your father's passing, and I don't see why I shouldn't do this—while I am still young enough to enjoy it."

"Fantastic. *Je te félicite.* And you want some advice on what to put in it?"

"That, and about nuts and bolts of the cellar itself."

"Fine. I'm warming to the whole dinner idea, Mum. But I have one more requirement."

A short sigh. "What?"

"No Patti Page, no Dean Martin, no Johnny Mathis, no Rosemary Clooney. No Sinatra. And no Windham Hill, either, now that I think of it."

Clearly annoyed, she abruptly blew cigarette smoke into the receiver. "You truly are my own personal despair."

"So we have a deal?"

DINNER WITH THE FAMILY

Afterwards, Brewster told himself the dinner could have been worse. Mum cooperated by having some chamber music on the sound system and by telling Corinne to open a third bottle of '78 Puligny Montrachet "Les Gonades" just when he was panicking at the sight of the second empty bottle and realizing they hadn't yet gotten around to the business items. He wasn't nearly drunk enough yet.

They sat in the small dining room—creaky walnut floor, a couple of knock-off Flemish tapestries on the walls, nice old crown moldings. Best of all was a generous bay window with a view of the Golden Gate. Brewster sat on one side of the table, Jock and Carolyn on the other, with Mum at the head.

As they worked their way through the coulibiac and haricots verts, Jock was still talking about Carolyn's promotion. "You have to appreciate the context of the story here. Carolyn is not just the youngest—and most beautiful—" (winking at her) "astrologer at B of A here in the city, but the youngest Senior Astrologer *ever* in the bank's history. And yes, she is that good." He reached over and massaged her shoulder.

Jock could have been mistaken for a banker himself. A

gym-tuned body in Turnbull and Asser suit, and tassel loafers. Short brown hair teased up with gel to look like a choppy sea. A freckled, heart-shaped face a bit like Brewster's, yet with more intense, predatory eyes and jaw, like his father's. Was he a tragic figure? Probably. He seemed to League members like a motivational speaker with questionable motives. For many years, when they referred to him at all, they identified him as "Shit-For-Brains." Carolyn was the "Bride of Jockenstein." She got as close to being a kewpie doll as was possible in this life: short, fleshy, round face with huge dimples, wispy blond hair. A ruthless positive thinker, her high voice often rose to a squeak when enthused, which was often.

"So!" Jock said, laying down his knife and fork. "Before we get to the super cool news about our catalog items, I want to be sure my wife knows what a gem she is. And that *you* guys know what a gem she is. I was so stubborn for so long about the whole idea of getting computers for the business, but damn, I'm telling you now how wrong I was. She nagged me into getting 'em—well, I don't mean 'nagged.' Not in a bad way."

"I encouraged you," said Carolyn.

"Right, exactly. Encouraged. Anyway, they're great. I should have figured if they were good enough for the banking community, they'd be ultra-cool for us. Our inventories? More accurate than ever. And they update like lightning. We just traded up to this new thing—what's it called again, honey?"

"Windows Excel."

"Whatever. It's outrageous! An accountant's wet dream, I swear. We're going to keep an eye on the 'internet,' too, as it develops. Big changes in the world of communication, and Spodie International'll be in the vanguard, for certain." He looked at Brewster. "How is your computer working out, Nipper? Good for your notes, your writing, whatever it is you do?"

"Yeah. Yeah, it's nice. Thanks for asking."

"Anyway. Moving on. Let me introduce you guys to the newest products in our book this fall, on the 'Spodie Debutantes' page. We're keeping it iconic! These beauties are going to convince those damn industry analysts that we are not some crappy little company with a build-and-exit strategy. And they'll never be able to say we're underexposed in specialty drinks again. Exhibit A! An apple-based product that's already gotten great ink in *The Guzzler* and a couple of other industry rags. It comes from Hoochworks, so we're in feel-good mode already. A great track record. They're the guys down in Gainesville Florida who had such a hit with the bourbon-based specialty, 'Trailer Mash'—remember that one? From a couple of years back? Anyway, this one's called 'Shiv! For a Stab of Flavor.' Great stuff! It comes in a jump-suit-orange sixteen-ounce can, and it's going to fly off the shelves. And like that's not enough, our second big addition is from the best damn flavor chemists anywhere, the crew down at Kafka and Beckett in Modesto! It's called 'Bordelle, A Taste of Old Paris.' Perfection. Grape-based product with natural and theoretical flavors. Super sexy presentation, too—a pink frosted twelve-ounce longneck. A four-pack for a buck seventy-five on the shelf. This is a huge coup for relatively little guys like us. Right now, we've got exclusive California rights, but I'm—"

"Can we taste them?" said Brewster. "You must have samples."

Jock looked pained. "This isn't the place for that, Nip. I don't have them yet, anyway. Next week."

"Have you tasted them?"

"Nipper, listen. These products are sure-fire. Tasting? Please. But I'll send samples to you next week, just to make happy times. How's that sound?" He leaned back in his chair. "And now how about we look at some great ideas to make a good thing even better? While we're enjoying Bernadette's Bavarian cream."

Mum dabbed her lips with her napkin. "You have to credit Corinne for her hard work, dear. But yes, by all means, let's. I'm dying of curiosity."

"Okay, so. Are you ready for this, my man?" he said to Brewster with a little smirk. Brewster had just poured himself another glass of wine, and gestured an unsmiling toast to Jock in response.

"Right, so let's talk flagship. Isopropov! Doing phenomenally well as you'll see when you get a look at the new spreadsheets. But the question is, what can we do to broaden its appeal to casual drinkers? What'll get us into broader demographics, like more affluent and educated groups? I'll tell you what. *Healthier* vodka! All the statistics point to greater health consciousness across the country, and we need to capitalize on it. So I am proposing a new vitamin-enriched Isopropov! Can you see this? I am talking a redesigned label with lots of color. You know— 'New! Now packed with vitamins and minerals!' And we put a short notice on the back about how five or six shots a day provide the drinker with 100 percent of his MDR of—-you pick the list—vitamin B-1, B-12, calcium, cesium. Vitamin F! Whatever!"

Brewster spoke up before he could stop himself. "You realize most any vitamin will taste repulsive in the vodka? They're not exactly flavor enhancers, even if they survive in alcohol and even if they're supposedly good for you."

"You're kidding, right? Nipper, Isopropov tastes like shit anyway, everyone knows that, ha-ha-ha. Small joke. This won't change things much—except to snare us a ton of new customers! I figure I'll have to come up with some lab people who can make sure the stuff doesn't get cloudy or something, in the bottle. But those are just details!"

Mum wore a troubled expression, looking down at her dessert.

"Okay, hang on. Let me put another idea out there. Talk about expanding our market. Now tell me, what is the single largest demo that has remained untapped for alcoholic beverages? It's kids! Of course! The five-through-fifteen bracket! And what I propose we do is nothing less than create a new label: Isopropov Junior. Or maybe 'Isopropov—for Kids!' You can already see the gold in them thar hills, right? I'm not talking about sixteens through twenties here: they've already created pathways to get a hold of the full-strength product. They're in the bag. No, I'm talking about your pre-school, elementary, middle school kids, the ones who dream of having a drink, just like mom and dad. So we market a product with half a percent alcohol—the actual volume doesn't matter as long as the government stays off our damn backs and we can still print a measurable volume somewhere on the package. We design a new label, you know, official and grown-up looking, with a mock seal on the cap, but with cartoon characters holding bottles of Isopropov, maybe Peanuts, maybe Looney Tunes—hey, maybe Marvel Comics! Love to get Disney, but that's a no go. They don't need us. But once we've got Linus or Foghorn Leghorn swigging from a colorful Isopropov kiddie bottle—we got 'em! And we back up the whole program with a one-two punch of a huge ad blitz on Saturday morning TV, then some lobbying muscle to get us into the Holy of Holies, the school cafeteria, right next to Coke and Mountain Dew!"

Brewster took a large, audible swallow of wine. Carolyn claps her hands and chirped, "Fabulous!"

"And you've had a look at the astrology on this, too, haven't you, pussycat?"

"I sure have, sweetie. But first I just have to say how delicious Corinne's dessert is. So scrumptious. We absolutely must be sure and validate her before we go. Anyway, I did chart a few progressions for the business, and there's no doubt we've got a couple of auspicious moments to launch these new ideas next spring, around April or May, I'd say. Lots of good energy for us here, with Jupiter in Aries and Mars in Gemini. You've got some beautiful aspects in the company's major progressions, too. Every bit as good as the ones that expanded B of A's foreign lending so amazingly a few years back." She giggled and hunched her shoulders. "I'm so excited!"

Mum leaned over and patted Jock's hand. "You know, dear, we all trust your judgment. I'm too old school to know much about the way business works nowadays, so I am always going to trust you. And I know Nipper agrees, don't you, Nipper?"

Taking another swallow of wine, Brewster nearly bit off the rim of the glass. "I, uh…I'm going to have to excuse myself. Need to do a pee." In the bathroom, he did a silent scream in front of the mirror. He splashed water on his face, slapping his meaty cheeks to relieve some of the exasperation.

Back at the table, the others had already begun to talk about mum's new wine cellar. They had decided it would be installed in the basement, in the same location as the old one, before Red had ordered it dismantled and all the wine sold, nearly fifteen years ago.

"I still can't understand why Pup would be such a meanie," Carolyn said. "He knew how thrilled you were with all those wines, didn't he, Mum?"

Corinne shuffled into the room just then and began collecting the dessert dishes.

"We'll have coffee here at the table, thank you, Corinne."

"Whatever you like." After twenty years working for the Hottes, she had an air of dignified resignation about her. Her graying chignon severe and perfect, her dark eyes blank.

"Super fantastic Bavarian cream, Corinne! It always blows my mind!" said Carolyn. With the barest hint of a smile and with stacked plates in her hands, Corinne bowed her head for a moment, then eased through the kitchen door.

"Your father had a temper, no doubt about that. I'd never say it outside of this room, but Isopropov did tend to make things worse—as you boys know. We heard all the reasons why the cellar had to go. But it's old business, and something I'm not especially fond of remembering. I'm going to have a cigarette now—I do not want to hear any comments."

Mum was referring to Red's periodic outbursts years ago, rants that eventually led him to have her basement wine cellar dismantled and the wines sold off. As Brewster had recounted to Margot on that special night in Bordeaux as he walked her back to her hotel, there had been cases of remarkable old Burgundies, Bordeaux, and Rhone wines. It had been devastating for Mum and Brewster, if not for Jock. Red had raged about Mum's abdication of wifely duties, none of which were ever specified. Why couldn't she just belong to a Canasta group or something? He was especially venomous about the stratospheric cost of wines that were obviously some kind of flim-flam put over on Americans by the French. He hated the French in general, from Maurice Chevalier to Giscard d'Estaing, whom he called "Discard G-string."

Brewster knew just how much more there was to it. He had seen the pleasure Mum took in learning a little bit about the wines, occasionally even keeping tasting notes. Though certainly not a wine devotee, she loved the beautiful labels, the ritual of opening bottles for special occasions and giving the boys small tastes. Red had never had any patience with it. Isopropov and Lucky Strikes had always been enough for him. Beyond that, only an occasional shot of bourbon in his coffee after dinner, or a huge vacation rum drink with a gardenia floating in it.

But all that was behind them as they sat around the table that night. Family trust money would be freed up to cover installing the cellar just where it had been before. Brewster would help Mum with the selection of wines—twenty-five to thirty cases to start.

"I would like to have some California wine as well," said Mum.

"Great idea, Mum," said Jock, with emphasis. "I've just been thinking there are enough interesting boutique operations out there that we ought to look at distributing some hand-picked ones. Not gonna be big revenue boosters, but good for prestige. And—and maybe we even get into an equity position with one or two, if everything works out." He massaged Carolyn's shoulder again, smiling. "And if the stars are right, of course!"

Awkward silence. Brewster waded in: "Anyway, a good idea, Mum. As long as you don't get any of these 'food wines' they talk about so much now. They're skinnier and nastier than Bernadette ever was. And—"

"Nipper! That is so unkind!" said Mum, in a haze of Benson and Hedges smoke.

"Sorry. Of course. No wine could ever be that nasty. Is there more coffee?"

Disgusted as he was with Jock's horror show of new products, and more ambivalent than ever on the question of dosing him, Brewster continued to use his influence in the League to block any such move. I flatter myself that I contributed modestly to that effort. Brewster despised Jock, yes, but punishing him with a ten-year dose of Zipp or MLII? He didn't have the stomach for it. And Dion and Hideo stood by him, though other key League members insisted that the situation was feeding cynicism and resentment in the organization. By omitting Jock from their targeting list because he was Brewster's brother, they asked, were the members endorsing the demi-monde of tasteless cretins who were their sworn enemies? What about principles? What about justice? What about *flavor*?

UNIVOD

Until early1990, the League had no understanding of the shadowy organization that controlled global vodka supply and distribution. It wasn't that we had bad intel: it was a case of virtually no intel. Like the rest of the world, we made assumptions when we heard the name "Univod." We assumed it was the Soviet government agency charged with that nation's vodka production, a nationalized collective of some kind. We knew nothing of its reach, nor its absolute political power. We had a lot to learn, and the process took longer than it might have. Why? Three main reasons. Most important was the fact that neither Univod nor vodka itself were perceived as especially objectionable in those days. It was a case of just another organization producing another form of alcohol. Univod was remote from League interests, too; it seemed far less important to research a distant organization than to target known individuals using vodka in nefarious ways closer to home, like the famous case of the Lithuanian living in Florida who in 1988 began selling a product called JiffyMist, 80% distilled water and 20% cheap vodka. Only slightly more expensive than regular distilled water, it was marketed primarily to women as "the REAL washday miracle," vaporizing in steam irons more quickly than water, offering "abundant fumes that say 'Have a Great Day!'"

The second reason was that Dion and the steering committee had placed the League's early focus on mid-level dirtbags and dipshits primarily in the wine industry, so that only in the late eighties did we begin to seriously ramp up operations against equivalent targets in the arena of distilled spirits. Though some members were unwilling to admit it, this broadening of emphasis was heavily influenced by Margot's increasing notoriety and her strident, very public campaign against vodka.

Last and perhaps most significant was the activity of Multishots, the international trade group and public face of vodka. At that time, the League erroneously believed that most vodka producers worldwide were discrete commercial entities and willing members of Multishots USA or one of its sister organizations, all with lavish budgets and offices in more than 100 cities around the world. But back then we also believed that the Soviet Union, soon to be the Russian Federation, was actually a conventional independent nation state among many others. We had a lot to learn.

At any rate, the smokescreen was being maintained then in brilliant fashion by Multishots USA's executive director, the tireless, charismatic sex bomb, Nadia Scrotova.

Depending on your viewpoint, Nadia was either a marketing and advertising genius, or a manipulative, cold-blooded whore. To my mind, she was no doubt both. Over a 20-year career that began in 1975, she compiled an amazing list of achievements, starting with her key role in shifting Martini aficionados from gin to vodka, the invention of landmark vodka cocktails like "Sex on the Beach" and "Long Island Iced Tea," and paving the way for the first brilliant cable TV spots for various upscale vodkas in the late nineties.

These were daringly elaborate productions featuring ice-queen models with brilliant red lips, glistening pyramids of Martini glasses flowing with crystalline, backlit vodka—all set to a throbbing Latin beat. Vodka consumption, already gratifyingly high, went through the ceiling.

Nadia was a svelt Amazon who came to New York City by way of St. Petersburg and an ancient, affluent American husband who, during their fleetingly happy time together, indulged her appetites while she indulged his. She lived in 5-inch heels. Her flowing blond hair contrasted with dark eyebrows hovering dramatically over steel-blue eyes and cheek bones that looked sharp enough to slash anyone who came too close. Without the benefit of hips or breasts, she managed to ooze sexual suggestion, though always with a dominatrix edge. A smile and a toss of her hair brought both men and women running to her side, just as she could freeze them in their tracks with an imperious lift of the chin and eyes void of recognition.

Most of the male League members lusted after her even when ugly rumors about her activities became a stigma. I remember even the irascible Impnitz looking at her across a hotel reception suite and sighing. "Hate the sin, not the sinner, right Vinnie? Didn't the Buddha say that? Or Jesus, or somebody?"

In hindsight, it is obvious that even without Margot's arrival on the scene, with her newfound notoriety and long-standing vodka grudge, other factors were converging as a serious test of Nadia's formidable talents. Her relationship with Jock Hotte, for one. And increasing League scrutiny, for another.

L'AMERICAINE MYSTERIEUSE

On an unusually warm day in early August, Brewster was sitting at his desk sipping a second glass of a wonderfully floral Savennières and entertaining vivid fantasies of lovemaking with Margot. Though the wine helped, he was as usual unable to see himself as the romantic lead in his own life-movie. He couldn't quite imagine himself supplanting some great bottle of Burgundy as the object of Margot's passion. He glumly began leafing through the latest edition of *WineSmut*, a hip, young trade journal. In the section "From France with Love," next to ads for wine-related sex toys and nursery rootstocks, he saw a quarter page picture of—was it possible?—a beaming Margot clutching some sort of golden wine bottle. The caption read: "American Foxes the French."

He pulled the page closer to his eyes. The short article reported that Margot had been a contestant on the French game show, *La Devinette*, and had swept her competition. "Of course!" Brewster said to the page. "Of course!"

Ms. Sipski became the all-time best performer on the show, a perennial favorite on French television station FR3. She succeeded in identifying all six wines presented to her in a blind tasting format, in each of four weekly segments, right down to places of origin, vintage years, and even the producers. This achievement, which the show's producers admit is unlikely to be equaled anytime soon, brought Ms. Sipski a purse of two and a half million francs, or USD520,000. Her tour de force performance, while welcomed as a vehicle for increasing viewership of the show, was also seen as an embarrassment for the French, in light of Ms. Sipski's American roots. Both her previous anonymity and her reticence to reveal details of her history have led devotees of the show to label her L'Américaine Mystérieuse, (The American Mystery Woman). All previous Devinette *winners have emerged from the ranks of somme-liers and wine professionals who had built solid reputations in the industry.*

The squawk box on his desk buzzed. Brewster punched the intercom switch. "State your business."

"Hey, Brew. It's me, it's the Bat. Open up."

Heidi Batschmitt rumbled through the door like the small tank she was. A five-foot, chunky bundle of energy originally from New Jersey, she talked and thought as fast as she moved. Her frizzy brown hair sat on her head like a small tattered umbrella. She usually skipped makeup, but her expressive mouth and mannish eyebrows still gave her face powerful animation. Many League members remember Brewster more than once saying he could have done with less animation from Heidi, and certainly less bubble gum, which she chewed constantly. But he had nothing but praise for her work as a relentless, bulldog private inves-tigator. She had been his choice for that work since 1984, when they met at the end of the annual Zinfandel tasting in

San Francisco, called Zindurance, at Fort Punter's Chugfest Hall near the Wharf. The League had assigned Brewster to attend, both to increase his exposure to California wine and have him scout out any scumbag operations worthy of targeting. Though he grumbled that other agents would be more suited to the job, ("Why not send Impnitz? He'd love this stuff.") he finally agreed to go.

Unfortunately, he had not understood the ground rules of Zindurance, though the name should have tipped him off. All doors were guarded by large and humorless male staffers, and once a participant had registered, paid, and entered the hall, departure was not permitted until all 200-odd Zinfandels had been tasted. At the door he received a tasting booklet and a small backpack emblazoned with the logo of one of the larger participating wineries. Each page of the booklet had to be signed off by the person pouring wine at each table, so that no wine could be skipped. The backpack contained materials to sustain the individual through the ordeal: bottle of water, three half-baguettes, smelling salts.

He had taken note of Heidi just as he finished with Table 28. He saw her plant what appeared to be a martial arts kick squarely in the crotch of a man standing at the remains of the food table, arguing with her about the last three cubes of Pepper Jack cheese and the last decorative bunch of seedless grapes. Brewster lurched over to her and introduced himself, both of them bleary-eyed, with blackened lips and teeth. She gave him a piece of cheese. "This tasting. Jesus, I can't believe I did this to myself," she said. "I'm no wine pro, I just thought it'd be fun. And then I find out I'm drinkin' stuff with enough alcohol to bring down an elephant."

"I know just how you feel," Brewster murmured. "And the tannins close in on your tongue like Nazis at Stalingrad."

By the time they finished the last table (#33), he had learned she was a Navy vet and a Taekwando 6th dan black belt. Best of all, she had studied Criminology at SUNY Albany and had five years on the street as a private investigator. Brewster told her only that he was a freelance wine and spirits writer who sometimes needed PI work done. It was the beginning of a productive business arrangement and a cockeyed friendship.

"Hey! Just take a look at this," he said, slapping the open magazine in her lap as she dropped into the chair next to his desk.

"Oh yeah," she said. Yeah, that *is* her, isn't it? Couldn't miss that Lone Ranger eye makeup." She flashed him a smile, snapping her gum. "Hey, for a minute there I thought you were tryin' to sell me some weird-ass sex toys. So who is this chick, anyhow? Why are you so interested? If you don't mind my askin'."

"Uh, I do mind, actually. What have you got for me?"

"Hey bub, I just hope *you* got a nice fat check for *me*, cuz I earned it. Swear to God." She slid a thick manila envelope toward Brewster. "How was France anyhow?"

"Lovely, really wonderful, as usual."

"But nothin' you can tell me about, I know, I know."

"Now you don't actually want to hear about visits to wineries and boring banquets in Bordeaux, do you?"

She gave him a vaudeville-pensive look. "Nah. Nah, probably not. But you could offer."

"I can offer you a glass of this delicious Savennières, how about that? If you get rid of your gum, that is."

She grinned, plucked the gum off her tongue and stuck it to the edge of Brewster's desk calendar. "Shit, you know me. I'll drink anything."

Brewster looked disgusted, his eyes on the wad of gum.

"Ah, come on, Brew. Just tear off that corner and dump it! You're not even going to miss the thirty-first of the month."

As Brewster disposed of the gum and began looking through the contents of the envelope, Heidi got a glass from the kitchenette. "You got enough stuff there for one bitchin' story, lemme tell ya. I practically got Margot's underwear size in there."

"Hmm. Looks good. Who is this guy Fudgy Ferjulian?"

"Oh yeah. Guy was kind of a dickweed. But I hadda take what I could get. Margot's mom's been dead for more than ten years, and her dad didn't leave much spoor out there. Couldn't find a trace of him after he moved from 29 Palms. He did a lotta long days in card rooms, I think. Not much for workin'. The cassette I put in there has all the interview stuff I could get about him from Fudgy. I used my cool new bogus L.A. Times ID, and the guy was so anxious to talk he was fallin' off his barstool."

"So how about a quick overview?"

"Sure. The headline is, Margot had a pretty gnarly childhood. Stepdad drank a lot—cheap vodka mostly—mom being kinda blind to it. Stepdad used to bring his drunk buddies back to the house late so he could get Margot out of bed and make her play bartender for 'em. He was, like, showin' off how he'd taught her to make Cosmos, Old Fashioneds, Stingers—shit like that. And according to numb-nuts Fudgy, she was really good at it. And this was around 1965 or '66? She was about 8 years old, for fuck's sake. He said she cried sometimes while she was mixing. Pretty sad."

"What else?"

"Basic stuff. Only child, lived with her mom in different apartments around Fresno and Kingsburg. Worked in a car wash, and then in a coffee shop as she went through high school. Good student. Wanted to be a large-animal vet, but couldn't handle the sight of blood. Not so clear how she ended up in the wine thing."

"Boyfriends?" Trying to sound casual.

"You kidding? With tits like that? There were four or five, you got the list there. But it only lasted 'til she got into her second year of the wine program—I love that part, they call it 'fermentation sciences.' Like 'wine guzzling' wouldn't sound so good. But yeah, it was weird, she dumped her current squeeze then without givin' him a reason. No sign of any kissy-kissy after that. I talked to that last guy—it's on the second cassette you got there."

Reading the rest of the article, Heidi whistled softly. "That's fat money for drinkin' a few glasses of wine. Hey, I think I qualify for the job!"

Brewster finally gave Heidi her check and sent her off, saying he would contact her with another job soon. Sitting at his desk, looking over the old photos of Margot and her family that were in Heidi's envelope, he was puzzled. Why would Margot decide to be a contestant on *La Devinette*? She always shunned the limelight, she was downright *shy*. And how did she manage to be selected as a contestant, anyway? Even an American who was well-known would have a tough time getting a slot on the show. What was going on?

TRACKING MARGOT

The next morning Brewster was at his desk before eight, effectively the middle of the night for him. He got on the phone to the only lead he had as to Margot's whereabouts: Domaine Butschling in Alsace, where Margot had told him she might work during the '90 harvest. Luckily, he got Alphonse, Butschling *père,* on the line and not his glitzy, slippery son. He told him he was trying to contact Margot to do a story about her big win on *La Devinette*, which was true as far as it went. Alphonse said she was not there, and gave him the Paris number of Juliénas Morgon, the girlfriend she had said she would be staying with. Brewster tried the number, got an answering machine. He left a message in English. "This is an old friend of Margot's, Brewster Hotte? Margot, this is an invitation to come to San Francisco to step on my hand. Either that, or have dinner. I know you're celebrated and famous now, but you can call me and still be celebrated and famous. 415-665-4133. *A bientot.*"

Surprise. She called back within an hour.

"Well this is a pleasant shock," said Brewster, straining to use his heartiest voice. "I thought you'd be out buying happiness. Or at least a new car or something."

"So you heard about it. Kinda thought that was why

you called. Have you been doin' okay?" He noted that she actually sounded like his answer would matter to her, and it flustered him.

"No. Yes, no, I'm doing well, thank you. But I called to congratulate you. Fantastic news, though I can't say I'm surprised."

"It was an interestin' experience, I gotta say. Those France-3 television people are totally looney-tunes."

"So why did you do it? If you don't mind my asking?"

"You're not writin' anything about me, right? This isn't some kinda damn interview? I never know what you're up to, Brewster, I swear."

"Well, to be honest, I'm getting together a nice feature about you for *The National Intoxicator*. But I'm willing to talk off the record here, if that's what you want."

"That's exactly what I want. All this publicity stuff gives me the willies. You know, in the last week alone? I've gotten a dozen calls for interviews, some even lookin' for product endorsements. Buncha bullshit."

"So you're doing them, right? Unless you're protecting your media virginity or something."

"Hell no, I'm not doing 'em. I told you how I feel about that crap."

"But why did you do the show? Was it love? Boredom? Patriotic fervor? Come on, we're off the record."

"Okay. I'm gonna trust you. Stupid me. But I swear I'll strangle you with your own bowtie if you sell me out."

"That kind of thing gets my hormones going, actually."

"Brewster! Cut it out. The deal is this: While I was workin' at the Butschlings, in Alsace? I found out they were havin' big money troubles. Fabrice didn't wanna talk about it, but I could tell. Then, toward the end of my stay, last January, he told me about *La Devinette*, the prize money, the whole deal. He said one of the producers was a friend of a friend and that he was sure he could get me a slot as a contestant, even bein' an American and a woman to boot. He was pretty shame-faced askin' me, but he wanted to know whether if I won I'd be willin' to loan 'em somethin'. Well hell, I told him I'd just *give* 'em money if I won anything. I—"

"Wait a minute, you mean you *gave* Fabrice Butschling a couple of million francs?"

"No! Course not. I gave him a million. I figured the rest would come in handy for some new jeans, maybe an apartment. Some cases of nice wine. Though that part is funny, because now cases of bodacious wine are showin' up at my friend Juliénas's door practically every day, from producers all over France. Some just from people who watched the show. It's nuts."

"Margot, tell me you're not in love with that grease ball."

A testy sigh. "Jeeesus in Bermuda shorts. You're not hearing me, are you? I told you over and over. I'm in a hot and heavy relationship with wine. And I don't leave out a nice Calvados or Armagnac or single malt once in a while, okay? What else can I say?"

"You could tell me you don't find me repulsive and that a modest spare tire on a man can sometimes be sexy. My hormones need to hear from you."

"Your hormones have shitty hearing. I think you're a kick, Brewster, you're a great guy. You're smart, you're funny, you don't seem to need smackin' with a two-by-four very often. What the hell do you want from me?"

"I'd settle for your exclusive, undying devotion." *And your body*, he thought.

"Damn, but you're crazier'n a rabid squirrel. I give up. So what else do you need for this interview? I'm not givin' out much stuff about my boring history."

He cleared his throat. "Well, Margot, I'm not going to sneak around. I kind of decanted that wine already."

"You *what*?" Margot erupted when he told her about the PI information he had, especially the recollections of her dad's old friend, Fudgy. Pictures from old Clovis High and Fresno State yearbooks were also considered foul play. She in fact called him a son of a bitch and a shitbag. He managed to calm her down by promising to include in the article a section about her *cause célèbre*, her one-woman anti-vodka movement. Also—and against his better judgment—he agreed to send a draft of the article to her by fax, and let her make some changes "within reason."

"Within whose reason?" she demanded.

"Mine. I think I'm a little more reasonable," he said. As he hung up the phone, he felt a thrill of excitement: he was becoming a real presence in Margot's life.

FAME WITHOUT SEX

It is difficult to be sure why Margot returned to Northern California in October of 1990, but one major factor was certainly the amount of hounding she received from the media and wine industry figures during her stay in Paris following her success on *La Devinette*. Brewster's recordings of three phone calls attest to her frustration and anger at the intrusions she was forced to endure. In retrospect, of course, we know just how horribly mistaken she was in the belief that she would have a lower profile in the United States; it would not take the media long to discover her. Another contributing factor, also borne out in conversations with Brewster and others, was a growing sense that her work in France was done. She felt pulled to return to California and undertake a more serious survey of an industry that was growing rapidly.

Brewster was in a state of agonized excitement over her promise to make San Francisco her home base, at least temporarily. He tried to adopt a casual tone in his conversations with her, but the recordings demonstrate how badly he failed in that effort. He needn't have worried: things fell into place almost miraculously. He was able to offer her one of his rental units on 24th Street that had recently been vacated, a decent apartment above generous office space, a block away from his similar office/flat. He convinced her to receive her burgeoning wine collection—upwards of four thousand bottles —into the wine storage warehouse south of Market Street where he stored most of his own wine. We also know that Margot had been in contact with several of her old friends from Fresno State, who were working winemakers in Slobova and Foppo counties. A handful of consulting-winemaker jobs had been floated, but Margot seemed unenthusiastic. "Gotta get my feet on the ground first," she had said to Brewster.

Brewster was in full fussing mode when Margot arrived, as San Francisco moved through a long series of cool, clear autumn days. He found furniture for her flat, toured her around the neighborhood, pointing out the best places for gourmand necessities: The Caffiend, The Butterfat Bakery ("the best chocolate *religieuses*!"), the Sign of the Beast for meats and charcuterie. He even managed to lure her to Union Square, where he bought her some new clothes. The outing was presented to her as "walking around a bit" before having dinner at La Gueule, a swank restaurant where Brewster swore she would be served the best *feuilleté* she had ever had. They ended up at Macy's well before their 7:30 reservation.

"And I'm not supposed to feel insulted, is that the deal?" Margot said, as he held up an orchid cashmere pullover and a white cotton blouse with navy pinstripes.

"Why wreck the moment by being difficult? Go with the flow on this. My treat. It's part of the personal Welcome Wagon package." He avoided eye contact, busily examining his choices. "So, we go with these. Perfect. Let's go look at jackets."

"I know how this works, Brewster. First they come for my jeans, then they come for my eyeliner."

"Come on! Why so negative? With all these great choices in front of you? God, Bernadette would have cleaned off a couple of racks and stripped all the mannequins in ladies' sportswear by now."

"I can never tell if you're a really generous guy or a connivin', manipulative asshole. At the moment I'm leanin' toward the latter."

"I'm a delicate blend. Just remember, if dropping all these clothes on the floor right now meant you'd get physical with me, we could walk right out of here and get a room."

"Okay, I gotcha," she said. "Let's get the clothes."

Margot recovered amazingly quickly from the inevitable culture shock, though she remarked to him more than once about the "sheer velocity" of her new environment. To explore the new California wine landscape that had emerged while she was in France, she agreed to take some day trips with Brewster, but also set up a daily tasting schedule for herself, to evaluate groups of wines themed on geography or grape variety. He offered to pay for the wines if he could taste with her; she refused, but invited him to taste as often as he liked. Brewster ran from mother-henning her to meetings with his mother about the selection of wines for her new cellar, at the same time quizzing her about how Jock's new products were being received. To his dismay, the answer was: pretty well.

He finished his *National Intoxicator* piece, which he titled "The Royal Palate: All Hail Queen Margot!" He counted himself lucky that she insisted on only a few changes: the removal of what to him was an endearingly awkward photo of her in the eighth grade, but one which she pronounced "dorky and humiliating;" and an expansion of the three lines Brewster had dedicated to her anti-vodka sentiments. Instead of being "unenthusiastic about vodka in general," she insisted on being described as a "ferocious anti-vodka partisan" who would always prefer tap water over "the scam-artist swill that vodka represents". He felt both fear and glee as he thought of Mum and Jock reading those phrases under his byline. He was ready to shrug and remind them that he wasn't being interviewed—Margot was.

The calls began as soon as Margot's office phone was installed. Her answering machine was immediately crammed with every kind of endorsement request, from importers like Twelve-Step Wines ("Surrender to a Higher Quality!"), to less obvious choices like the disposable towel maker Bernie's Wipeouts (Handles the sloppiest wine taster) and cosmetics by The Grateful Goth. There were appearance requests, too, for restaurant openings and cable cooking shows.

"This is gonna make me crazy. What do I do?" she asked Brewster.

"Get another line, an unlisted number. And another machine."

"I just can't believe this is happening."

"You mean you can't believe that Americans are wretched, soulless, moneygrubbing jackals, is that it? Or that you're a media star now?"

"I mean I didn't think wine was such a big deal in America. I thought it was all about Rambo and beer and bourbon. Or…somethin'."

"Come on, Margot, seriously? You were around for the Slag's Heap tasting in Paris. Wine was exploding in America even before you finished school. Just get used to this. It can be managed. I'll help you."

"That's what I'm afraid of."

By March of 1991, Margot had given in to the whole idea of fame and was a wine industry headliner. Her schedule was crammed, her bank account swelling, her fame growing. She did tasting demonstrations at theater venues for four-figure compensation, and product endorsements, too, for everything from wine glasses to peanut butter. In February alone, she initiated agreements with Senior Soakers adult briefs and Fidofill dog food. There was no question of her taking a winemaking job. Why would she? She was even beginning to think she needed to sideline Brewster and get a real agent.

He hated doing a puppy-dog routine, but he pleaded with her anyway. "Weren't you the one who wanted to steer clear of the limelight when you came to San Francisco? What happened to that person? Margot, you should stick with your friend on this. The friend you won't let do more than give you a hug, but who's slavishly loyal and would never try to cheat you like all the sharks out there in the world. You know: him. That guy." She finally agreed to stay the course with Brewster, though she admitted there were now phrases going around in her head, like "percent of the gross" and "stock participation."

At each event, Margot took time to bash vodka. Sometimes she sprinkled pot shots in her tasting remarks ("This wine is vodka's little cousin, with a 'hospital corridor' character in the nose, and a huge lucky shot of anesthetic on the palate—just in time to keep you from tasting much of anything. Best tasting note? Probably, 'It gets you drunk'"); or she dedicated time to savaging it directly ("I want to take a minute here to remind you why any serious taster would never bother with the sensory deprivation, drunk-driven non-pleasures of vodka. It leaves you clueless!").

She fought with Brewster more often now, too. Not just about the tone of the anti-vodka crusade—though that was always front and center—but also about her clothes, his alleged over- attentive style, and of course about their relationship.

"Where's the sex?" he demanded.

"What? What d'ya mean? I don't know where the sex is! Did you leave it in your other pants or somethin'?"

THE LEAGUE CONCLAVE, OCTOBER 1990

Two weeks after Margot's arrival in San Francisco, Brewster traveled to the League's Control Hub for its semi-annual conclave. On the first morning of the three-day gathering, Dion stood before us, the assembled members, clutching a clipboard of blank sheets. He smiled widely, eyes disappearing into pink slits. "As we are all aware, it has been a magnificent six months for us. Just magnificent. At times like this, I realize I don't need to try to make inspirational comments, because all of you have provided actual inspiration for each other, through your brilliant fieldwork. As Bobby Tillotson so aptly put it in his 1961 classic hit, 'Poetry in Motion': 'I love every movement/ there's nothing I would change/ she doesn't need improvement/she's much too nice to rearrange.' But there will be plenty of time to recognize individual heroes at the banquet. For the moment, we'll focus on where we're going, not where we've been.

"So. The state of our wine and spirits world. What have we got for despicable characters, those who really *need* our attention?" He wheezed a laugh. "Thus far this year we've put a lot of emphasis on lower-end American business—which is, of course, a treasure trove of terrible taste and skullduggery—but there are signs that we would be well served to shift some resources toward England and France, and perhaps, for the first time, even farther east. The Soviet bloc is essentially terra incognita for us, but we may soon need to be much more attentive to what goes on there, should communism's insular forms of bad taste give way to the more free-ranging and seemingly bottom-less bad taste which is capitalism's specialty." A thin smile.

"As always, the white board is here for your suggestions as to targets, in your own area of responsibility or in some other. The Steering Committee will have a list of confirmed operations for the coming quarter by Sunday morning so there will be plenty of time to air your objections. But I want to talk for a moment about the Royal Weenie. The topic came up before, you might recall, in 1988, when we briefly considered operations against particularly loathsome food service operations. I still believe it was the right decision to avoid involvement in food items, since we have our hands full already with wine and spirits issues. But now, by offering 187-milliliter bottles of wine nationwide, the Royal Weenie franchise has crossed the line and invited us into the fray. There is powerful justification for action in these totally re-pulsive red and white wines, both of which our lab confirms contain polymers commonly found in cheap hairsprays. And we have their new ad campaign as well, inviting all of us to 'Suck down some Royal Weenie—Red or White!' If you have input on the topic, please see agent Impnitz.

"Also this morning, I want to initiate a discussion about vodka. Now, in the past we have treated vodka as we treat any distilled spirit, that is, there are labels of higher quality, such as the Soviets' Blottoskaya and Sweden's Insolent; and lower quality ones, like Steer Kleer from Texas, and

Isopropov from California. No offense to agent Hotte, of course." Another lean smile. "But now we are confronting another idea entirely, the one popularized by the wine-tasting superstar, Margot Sipski. And that is, that all vodka is in poor taste and illegitimate in the family of alcoholic beverages."

Brewster sat, horrified, as he listened to Dion talk about all the reasons why Margot might be right. The pressure to act against Jock—maybe even Mum—was going to be huge if her ideas finally gained traction with the League. His family, such as it was, would be in the crosshairs. Dion went on talking about the sketchiness of vodka's merits, as if he'd already decided the question. He sounded like Margot, Brewster thought, talking about how both high- and low-end vodkas were a major ingredient in endless numbers of disgusting mixed drinks, many with names involving clumsy sexual allusions. It was all food for thought, Dion concluded, wearing the expression of someone who didn't like what he'd just eaten. "As the Buffalo Springfield reminds us in their 1967 hit 'For What It's Worth,' 'There's something happening here/ What it is ain't exactly clear.'"

Impnitz, seated in the row behind Brewster, muttered, "Finally we get around to Isopropov. *Finally.* You mean I'm not a voice crying in the fucking wilderness anymore? Break my heart. Really."

After the banquet that evening, when most everyone was in the screening room watching tapes of the TV series *The Avengers* (a League favorite), I sat with Brewster in one of the small auxiliary offices, letting him vent as we sipped some beautiful '63 Graham Port.

"It's looking brutal, Vinnie. Even with that beautiful

bourride in front of me at dinner, I could hardly eat anything," he said, shaking his head mournfully.

"I noticed."

"I've seen Dion put on his stern face before, but this time he was pushing pretty damn hard."

"Was it just the two of you? Where was Hideo?"

"Yeah, just the two of us. I think Hideo was meeting with the Rec Committee about changing our premium well drinks. I wonder if there's a move to drop vodka."

"So what happened?"

He looked at me and smiled wearily. "Good old Vinnie. Always helping out. You don't really want to hear all this stuff."

"Hey, Brewster. My friend. I know you, remember? You're going to tell me whether I want to hear it or not."

"Good point. Of course the deal is that he wants to dose Jock. And heavily, too. Not just because of Isopropov, which is still supposedly a debatable topic, but because of the other junk in the product line. He says the pressure from the Steering Committee is intense, and I get that; but I explained to him it isn't that simple. I know that if they dose Jock and he bows out of the company—which is not a certainty—Mum will just replace him with some sweaty, number-crazed, fascist MBA."

"Why don't you take over if Jock is out?"

"Ha. That's a laugh. First reason, Mum would never go for it. She knows I hate the whole thing. That's the second reason, by the way: I hate the whole thing. But like I told Dion, it's guaranteed that the new person will be more of an arrogant, tasteless dirt bag that Jock ever was, and I'll have less chance of influencing him."

"How much influence have you had on Jock?"

He sighed. "None. But maybe I could. Sometime."

I cleared my throat. "So what happens now?"

Brewster shrugged and sipped his port. "He tried to be positive and lighten the mood as we were finishing up. He said he would hold the line for now, but if the heat got much hotter, he couldn't guarantee anything."

"Well, that was good, wasn't it?"

"Yeah. Like an anvil hanging over my head is good." He smiled grimly. "He patted me on the back as we got up, and reassured me he was on my side. He said, 'I'm just a soul whose intentions are good. Oh lord, please don't let me be misunderstood.'"

I'd been in the League long enough to recognize song lyrics. "The Animals, wasn't it?"

"Right. 1965, according to Dion. He said it was Nina Simone, originally."

I couldn't help but chuckle. "God, I love the League."

"Don't we all. More port?"

The National Embarrasser — June 6, 1990

TEETOTALING ALIENS SPREAD GLOBAL TERROR

A mysterious plague has been stalking wine and spirits moguls across the globe for years now, leaving tragedy and broken lives in its wake. Victims of this scourge are left pleading for death as they undergo a nightmare of shattered nerves, loss of taste and smell, and emotional turmoil. What is this horrifying condition and where did it come from? More and more experts on extraterrestrial life think they have the answer.

Recovering alcoholic aliens.

According to Adrian Flicker, Chief Scientist at the Rodeway Inn in Roswell, New Mexico, there are at least three alien civilizations with scouting parties walking among us, two of them extremely hostile to alcohol production and consumption. Both of these have banned all alcoholic beverages on their respective planets, one because of the terrible social costs, the other because of what it does to their breath. One of these advance parties, he says, is certainly responsible for the pestilence that has caused so much misery in the world of booze.

How do they do it?

How can they be stopped?

How can they possibly hate a good beer?

Is Tom Selleck one of them?

All these questions and more have been treated in Flicker's new book, Intergalactic Temperance Wars, which he describes as a recipe for neutralizing these alien predators, and also for making stellar Singapore Slings, Rob Roys, and other classic cocktails.

"The fact that these creatures have been able to divert the attention of international law enforcement with fanciful theories about vindictive human vigilante groups leads me to suspect that Interpol itself has been compromised with alien presences," Flicker said. "It is more than suspicious that no one in its current administration drinks anything stronger than Fanta Orange. Our vigilance should be heightened by this news, our premium well drinks discounted, and our happy hours extended."

As to exactly what substances are being used in the attacks, he demurred, quoting the words of more than one American politician on the issue. "How should I know? I'm not a scientist."

Nevertheless, Flicker is bullish about the chances of ultimately apprehending these otherworldly criminals. "Don't worry, they're going to slip up. They'll tip their hand soon enough," he said. "Sooner or later, you'll hear about someone being a little too strident about the so-called 'social costs' of alcohol consumption. Then you'll nab them. That, or there will be a group that seems hell-bent on grabbing headlines by droning on about healthy beverages. A dead giveaway. Hopefully none of it will come down before my book gets to a second printing," he told us, in conclusion.

THE LUCKY WINNERS

A day tour of Foppo Valley with Margot. It was a master stroke, Brewster thought. Big benefits all around. It wasn't like she knew nothing of the valley and its wineries, but this was a chance to formally introduce a conquering tasting champion to the local wine community. It was also chance to massage some of his connections at the Wine Conflation, the industry's promotional arm, headquartered in San Francisco. He had let the Conflation people put the tour together, asking for an interesting mix of large and small, trendy and established wineries, to bring Margot up to speed with changes in the industry.

Even better, the tour was another way to cement his relationship with Margot. He had to make an effort not to look too contented. A beautiful late winter morning, the crackling sunlight already blunting the brittle air, driving up to wine country with Margot beside him. It was a fantasy he could hardly have imagined even a year before.

She was fidgeting in her seat.

Brewster patted her knee. "Just think of this as a victory lap, Margot. It's all good publicity for you, remember."

She grunted. "Publicity, yeah. How much is that crap worth, again?"

"The right kind of publicity is your fairy godmother, and you know it."

In the event, the tour served only to put Margot in a bad mood for a couple of days.

The first few visits should have been a warning. There was a stop at the new operation called Rapunzel Cellars, where they were herded to the "Hairlift," a sixty-foot tangle of thick, ropelike yellow nylon fibers to which they were harnessed, then winched to the top of the Rapunzel Tower, to enjoy the breathtaking view. Margot scowled through the arranged tasting in The King's VIP Dungeon, a tasting she later described as "lookin' behind some old dusty sofa cushions for whatever was stinkin' back there."

They visited two small places up near the crest of the Dannitomas Mountains, on the border with Slobova County, one of which produced wines packing 16% alcohol, which Margot pronounced as drinkable only if you were on a steady diet of "goddam bear steaks and moose pies." The second had a back-to-nature proprietor apparently so averse to bathing that tasting wine while standing next to him was problematic. "Natural wines are the goal!" he said. "The grapes need to express themselves. I just get out of the way and let 'em do it!" Back in the car, Margot said, "I kinda doubt that guy could get far enough out of the way."

Once down off the mountain, they headed north toward St. Rapina to have lunch. Margot was glum, and rejected Brewster's offer to play a Johnny Cash tape.

He was exasperated and a little defensive. "So, what do you want to do? You want to just go back to the city, bail out on the whole schedule? Piss off the rest of the people you were supposed to see today, and everybody at the Wine Conflation, too? Is that it?"

"Just drive. Don't worry about it." She looked straight ahead.

Only a couple of miles down the highway, Brewster saw flashing lights in his rear view mirror. "Oh Christ."

Margot craned her neck, looking back. "Is it the cops?"

Brewster reached over quickly and opened the glove box. He pulled out a silver flask, popped the cap and took a pull. He passed it to Margot. "Take a couple of swallows of this. Quick," he said, checking the rearview again. A patrol car was right behind them.

"What? Why? What is it?"

"Just *do* it. It's a '62 Armagnac. Slump down in your seat, and drink it! Hurry! When I pull over the guy'll be right on us."

He was just closing the glove box when a tall, pear-shaped figure of a man lumbered up to Brewster's window. His uniform was khaki and green, with impressively thick, creaky black leather belts around his waist and across his chest. His youthful pink complexion contrasted with his blond crewcut. His smile was easy, lots of teeth. "Do you know why I stopped you?"

Brewster knew. "Y'know, Officer, I—"

The officer's smile widened. "Well of course you don't! That's because you've been selected at random from motorists on the highway today to receive valuable passes for free tastings at some of the valley's finest wineries! This week's choices include the beautiful Castello Scarfo up in Caliponzi and the fabulous Ozzie Candyass Cellars, with its gorgeous hanging gardens, just south of Saint Rapina.

Be sure not to miss the spectacular Mustache Museum while you're there!"

Margot looked on, incredulous, while Brewster took the stack of brochures and coupons. "Well, thanks so much for this, um, officer. We'll be sure to have a look."

"Hold on, sir, we're not done yet. There's another little piece of business to attend to. I need to make sure you two are in the zone."

"The zone?"

"Yessir. Point-zero-three to point-zero-seven. Blood alcohol. That's what we need to see from drivers in the valley."

"I heard something about this, officer, but I wasn't clear on the exact numbers."

"Oh, they're exact, all right. Take a look here, on the back of a coupon—there you go—it's got the whole grid. Ounces of wine, your weight, the resulting alcohol in your bloodstream. If you are apprehended and you are out of the zone, you are subject to loss of your license, and comedy driving school without possibility of parole. It's the law."

Brewster could see Margot's jaw drop. "So we need to have at least a point-zero-three blood alcohol to be legal, is that it?"

"Exactly right, sir."

"Well, my friend and I have already enjoyed a couple of winery visits, so I'm sure we're in compliance."

"That's excellent, sir. I thought I smelled something good in the car here. Just so you're aware that a reading of less than point-zero-three, from any driver in the valley, is considered to be a gross lack of support for local wineries. A lack of appreciation of their products."

"I understand, no problem. But I have to ask, is this for local people—truckers. too?

The officer nodded vigorously. "Especially for those individuals. 'Cause they live here, they should be the most gung-ho of all. It's all about the general welfare. Clear?"

"Oh yes. Yes. Thanks ever so much."

The officer's huge smile bounced back. "Sure thing. And even though you guys don't seem nearly happy enough, I'm not gonna breathalyze you today; we'll just call it an informational warning. I hope you have a fantastic time in our beautiful valley! Enjoy!"

HOLY GROUND

"I wanted to bring you lovely people up here to show you just what holy ground looks like. I'll tell you, it's a humbling experience being custodian of viticultural royalty like this." Crispin Saggy, owner of the Saggy Estate above St. Rapina, smiled and squinted into the distance, gesturing across the immaculate patchwork of vineyards that led down to the valley floor. He wore a powder blue oxford shirt, sleeves rolled up to the elbow, and tailored khaki slacks. A tanned, vigorous fifty-something, you could picture him loping through the vine rows on one of his appaloosas, if not driving a tractor or pruning vines. "Like I always say to my Jewish friends who come to visit, this is kind of the Holy of Holies of planet earth's wine temple. Thirty-one acres of the finest vineyards in the world."

"Very beautiful," Brewster muttered. Out of the corner of his eye, he saw Margot's expression. Pure irritation. But he was determined to make nice; everything about the Saggy Estate oozed prestige, and he was prepared to lick some boots. Bernadette had always hated it when he was like this. Self-castration, she called it. He could still hear her voice: "You can be agreeable without fawning, you know. You're always cutting off your goodies and handing them over on a plate."

"This spot is California's Premier Grand Cru territory, full stop," said Saggy. "The best of the best. With the background you two have, you know all about the French cru system. Well, their wines are almost as good as ours!" He chuckled. "Over there to the left of that row of sycamores is the Robert Svengali property—nice wines, elegant wines. A little light for my taste. We're the powerhouse in this neighborhood." He lifted his chin, crossed his arms, and contemplated the horizon with a serene smile.

"Gorgeous," said Brewster, with feeling. "It makes sense that fantastic wine should come from such a fantastic spot."

Saggy smiled. "Roger that. We'll get you a barrel tasting of the '89 in a little bit. God, what would I have given to have some of these wines when I was a young buck in the fifties, living in the penthouse of the Artemis in Manhattan, with my houseboy, Victor. I was living like a king back then! But when it came to drinks, I didn't know there was anything beyond Dom Pérignon and Crown Royal. More's the pity."

"You're from New York, then?"

"Originally. But I came here by way of Houston. That's where Nellie and I met, and where my boys were born."

Margot turned to face him, cocking her head. "So tell me again? How long you folks had the vineyard?"

"We've been here three years now. But it feels like, I don't know, a homecoming of sorts. It's great to get back to the land."

"Back to the land?" Margot's lopsided grin was hard to read.

"Right. Not many people know it, but my dear old

grandad was one of the first shareholders in ConAgra. And my dad worked for twenty-eight years on the commodities exchange in Chicago. So it runs in the family. I feel like we're just coming full circle here. My boys are driving tractors and doing cellar work when they're on breaks from school. They'll be ready to take over from the old man pretty soon!" He chuckled again as he ushered them back up the trail to the winery.

As they tasted the impressively dark-colored Cabernet from the 1989 vintage, Crispin told them how gratified he was to have been accepted so readily by the local community. Everybody from the city council on down was thrilled with St. Rapina High's new Saggy Sports Pavilion and the Nell Saggy Performing Arts Center.

Back in the car, Margot was withering. "Why didn't you just glue your lips to his butt? Just because that guy can buy a new boat every time his old one gets wet. *C'est dégueulasse.*"

"What do you mean? I was respectful, as I should have been. As *you* should have been. That's a fantastic place! Did you see all those new barrels? That's a top-flight operation."

"Yeah, oh yeah. And he's real dedicated to his vineyards. I'm sure he loves watchin' his workers while he's sittin' in his pool, sippin' on some damn vodka drink."

The Cooper sputtered as Brewster nosed down the narrow road to the highway. "That's just not fair, Margot. He's doing a great service to California and the whole wine world by taking that property in hand and improving it. It's not like you don't have a good idea about how much money it takes to keep up a place like that. He's got big holdings in Oklahoma, and some in California, too."

"You don't have to tell me that. I saw his family name all over the place down around Bakersfield. I think his dad was the real big cheese. I don't think this guy's gonna hurt his back totin' his brains."

"So you do know about him."

"Sure. Love the irony, too. Guy pollutes the hell out of thousands of acres of Central Valley land so he can pay to keep up his 31-acre organic showplace in St. Rapina. Makes sense."

A low growling noise came from Brewster's throat as he drove. Sweet Jesus, he thought. If wine writers heard the stuff she was saying, they'd put pipe bombs in her mailbox.

NEWSFLASHES
THE NEW AVATAR OF TASTING: MARGOT SIPSKI

It's not every six-year-old who carries around a sterling silver tasting cup in a purple velvet drawstring sack. But then Margot Sipski, from Fresno, California, was no ordinary little girl. As the woman whose tasting skills humbled scores of misogynistic wine professionals on French national television, and who that same night went on to scatter a crowd of dangerous thugs at the studio door by landing solid haymakers on a couple of Gallic chins, Margot was destined to be an iconoclastic, trailblazing genius.

From the most unassuming beginnings, including a broken home and a few years of using old wine boxes to fashion crude shoes for herself, Margot remained true to her love of wine. Through a childhood spent singing and dancing for nickels—everything from "Mr. Bojangles" to "The Sound of Music"—at The Homewrecker, her stepfather's downtown Fresno hangout, she saved to buy the odd bottle of Bordeaux Supérieur or Beaujolais Villages. "I was mysteriously attracted to French wine, and hungry for knowledge," she told WFM. "Pretty thirsty, too." Instead of reading about Dick and Jane, she spent her early school years reading Alexis Lichine's Wines of France *and H.W. Yoxall's* Wines of Burgundy, *committing them both to memory by her first year of junior high school.*

Once she had two Fresno State University degrees under her belt, an MS in Fermentation Sciences and an MFA in Wine Consumption, she was off to France for a seven-year sojourn during which she familiarized herself with every inch of French viticultural territory.

With characteristic modesty, Margot describes her years working for some of the great stars in the French wine firmament as "laying a foundation." But her fabulous talents were evident to all from the get-go. During that time, she was not only offered numerous winemaking jobs in Burgundy's Cote d'Or and in the finest communes of the Bordeaux region, but also received offers to work as chef de cuisine at the prestigious Restaurant St. Prique in Paris, and as France's Deputy Culture Minister for Alcoholic Affairs. She turned them all down in favor of continuing her quest to understand the soul of French wine.

Today, the degree of her success can be measured by the hefty fees she receives for private tutorial tastings, demonstrations, and personal appearances, much of which are donated to the French branch of Snobisme Anonyme, the association that cares for those unfortunates who abuse the finest wines in an attempt to appear sophisticated. She is esteemed by internationally known wine figures such as Jules Monetizeur, Diplomate of the Brussels Liver Exchange, who told us: "Be damned if I know how she can identify all those wines. In the fifteenth century, she'd have been burned at the stake."

Margot continues to amaze us, and, through her example, has inspired a whole new generation of young people who are drawn to the art and science of drinking.

BREWSTER EXPOSED

One morning in mid-March, Brewster's phone rang. He picked up and heard a wispy, feminine voice: "We'll do the Twist, the Stomp, the Mashed Potato too, any old dance that you want to do, but let's dance."

So. Another assignment, beyond the quarterly schedule of operations. This one local, involving two targets.

"Gonna give you every inch of my love," he replied, signifying his acceptance as well as his agreement to travel to a neutral site for more instructions.

As was so often the case, I was tasked with handling logistics for him. We were to meet in Reno, and Brewster was gracious enough to suggest getting together at Gimpy's, a downtown motel coffee shop. As he toyed with his scrambled eggs and I enjoyed the guilty pleasures of a plate of Sloppy Joes *au jus*, we ran through the particulars of the job that would occupy him until the first week of April. Intel had gotten wind of an idea floated by the owner of an exclusive Foppo Valley winery to a Japanese producer of the prestigious Daiginjo sake: a joint venture creating a blended product to be called "Chardonnaki," under the label "Rising Sun, Golden Bear." The League Steering Committee had assigned Shithead status to both targets.

Brewster expertly wangled an invitation to both the joint

press conference and reception in San Francisco, where the principals would be present. Anticipation was high at the Control Hub, but, tragically, Brewster botched yet another mission. And how galling that his failure could so easily be traced to his old nemesis: top flight, rare wines. At the reception, where he had planned to strike, there were not only dozens of wait staff circulating with trays of *canapés*, but also, unfortunately, tables offering excellent old vintages of France's most famous Chardonnay, Le Montrachet, from producers like Bonair, Lafoney, and the Marquis de Pastiche. A sign over the tables read "Chardonnaki Honors the Past—and Reaches for the Future." After less than an hour, Brewster found himself honoring the past by kneeling in a men's room stall and repeatedly testing the toilet's flush function.

The aftermath at the Control Hub was even grimmer than it might have been, because of the presence of Impnitz on the Debriefing Committee for calendar 1991. "How was the wine, Hotte? I'll bet it was great," he sneered. "Hope you didn't get any puke in the cuffs of those nice pants of yours!" Completely deflated, Brewster offered no defense. He kept his eyes down and sipped his Badoix water while Dion explained to him that he would be suspended from League activity for a year. It was a huge blow, and something that had not occurred since 1983, when an operative missed what turned out to be the only chance to dose Hosea Klime, the creator of Sir Loin's Meaty Mighty Red Wine (With Real Beef on the Bottom!), before he sailed off to his private, heavily guarded south sea island.

Back at home, a steady drizzle soaked the city. The sky was as low as his spirits; all the umbrellas on 24th Street were black. Thoroughly drenched, he dragged himself and his bag up the stairs to his apartment, thinking how much he wanted to see Margot. In the run-up to this operation, he had not done any tastings with her—he hadn't seen her at all, in fact.

Sitting at his desk, listless, staring at nothing, Brewster sank deeper into his own psychic sludge. He couldn't find the energy to get himself a glass of something decent from his wine cabinet. He was finished. Why write articles? Why bother doing tastings? Even: Why call Margot? He struggled to get his keys out of his pocket, opened the bottom desk drawer. He pulled out a small orange plastic container saved from some long-ago pharmacy visit. In it was nearly a half inch of very fine white powder, an unholy mix of Zipp and MLII that he had painstakingly collected, bit by bit, from previous operations. Hoarding of what the League called "ordnance" was strictly against protocol and, had any members known, would have gotten him banished for life. Yet following most operations, he had not completely emptied his signet ring or his cufflinks, as regulations demanded. In his mind, it was a little hedge. For emergencies. But now he was horrified to realize that he was seriously thinking of dosing himself. Why not? He was of no value to the League now. Too unreliable, too undisciplined, too addicted to great wines. Even after he returned to active membership, he would carry the stigma of his failure, his weakness. So why not solve the problem by robbing himself of taste and smell for ten years or so, and give away most of his vodka-generated Hotte family assets, too? It would be an unburdening, a solution of sorts.

What he didn't realize was that while he had been gone, working his way toward this disaster, a couple of other disasters had ripped through his world, too.

The first of them detonated when, after several solo tasting sessions, Margot invited one of her old Fresno State friends, Mitzy Quoff, to join her one morning. Mitzy was muscular, freckled, outspoken. They tasted twenty-two Necrocino County Cabernets that morning, afterward lunching at the nearby cafe, the Coup de Food.

"Thank God for some white wine," said Mitzy, between bites of her chicken *paillard*. "Thought I was gonna need a belt sander to get those tannins off my tongue. Polite people talk about Necro Cabernet as 'rustic.' You can imagine what the rude ones like me say." She took another swallow of wine. "So how is it now, being famous and all?"

"Not much better here than in Paris."

"Excuse me?"

"It's true," said Margot, hoisting a forkful of lamb stew. "After I was on the show the first couple of weeks, the attention got pretty annoyin', gettin' stopped on the street and all. Wine's such a big deal in France, I felt like I couldn't have a life. In this country—and you know this as well as I do—there'd never be a national TV show about wine. I figured there'd never be a big whoop about some woman who's a good taster, but the joke's on me. I'm busier than a funeral parlor fan in summer. All kinds of calls to do demonstrations and endorsements and stuff. It's cuttin' into my beauty sleep. But I'm gettin' to taste lots of interestin' wines. And since an old friend in Paris—you remember Juliénas, don't you?—is shippin' me pallets of wine from a bunch of French producers that want me to taste their new releases, I kinda have the best of both worlds." She smiled and shrugged. "So I'm dealin' with it."

"You're place is really nice. It's a kick-ass thing, having your office downstairs from your apartment."

"Yup. It's real comfortable. My friend Brewster Hotte has some rental units around here, and he offered me one. You know Brewster?"

Mitzy's chewing slowed. She sipped her wine, looking perplexed. "I don't know the guy personally. But I know something about him. I kind of wondered how you ended up with him, honestly."

Margot's faint smile made an appearance. "What's it to ya?" She reached over and smacked Mitzy's arm playfully. "No big deal. We're not screwin' or anything, trust me. He's just a good friend."

"It's not that. I just…couldn't make sense of it. You, always being so down on vodka and all."

"What d'you mean?"

"You know about Spodie International? The company started by Brewster's father, I guess? It's a big importer and distributor."

"Hang on a minute. Is Brewster tied up with that shit-hole company?"

Mitzy rolled her eyes. "Oh boy. I'm putting my foot in it now. You know about their big cash cow, Isopropov?" She looked away, hesitating. "Jeez, I hate to be the one to lay all this on you—"

So the whole story came out. Margot did not finish her meal. Mitzy could see the dark cloud form over her head, and left right after lunch. Back at her desk, Margot called Brewster's office and left a message, her voice shaking with rage:

Brewster, I should probably be readin' from a prepared statement just to keep from losin' it. But this is gonna be a short message anyhow. You bastard. You fucker. You really had me goin'. My stepdad used to say I'm about as sharp as mashed potatoes, and maybe he was right. But now I've sharpened up a little. I know about your family and that shitty, cheap vodka you make. And I know you're gonna have some bullshit story to smooth it all over. But I want to tell you: forget it. The only thing I wanna do is talk to you about is how fast I can get out of your fuckin' rental unit.

TRULY EUNUCH WINES

She was still sitting at her desk, cursing Brewster under her breath, her mind a typhoon of revenge and escape plots, when the phone rang. It was disaster number two, none other than Fabrice Butschling, whom she had not heard from since she left France.

"*Ca va, ma chérie*? I 'ave miss you," he said.

"*Oui, en gros, ça va, ça va*. Thanks. Where are you? Are you home?"

"No, no. That's just eet. I am in Paris now, but I come to San Francisco tomorrow. I want to see you!"

Margot agreed to have lunch with him, thinking spiteful thoughts of Brewster. During her *stage* at the Butschling *domaine*, Fabrice had extracted nothing more than regular hugs from her, though he was clearly interested in something more. So why not fool around now, if there was an opportunity? He was charming and hunky, and, well, hadn't she been a wine nun long enough? Extra bonus: it would cause Brewster pain.

Fabrice said he had exciting news. Lots to talk about, potentially great things for everyone. He didn't want to spoil the surprise. She insisted it would just be nice to see him again and to talk. "*Bien sur!*" he said.

Two days later, she showed up before noon at the

Coup de Food. She was not sleeping well since the revelations about Brewster, so she was a little dazed as she sat waiting for Fabrice. He swept in, fifteen minutes late, all smiles and apologies, wearing a white pullover that showed off his inexplicable Alsatian winter tan. He carried a sturdy canvas sack. They exchanged *bises*, he swore she was more beautiful than ever, his white teeth glowed. After they caught up on the news about the '90 wines at the Butschling estate, he pushed back from the table and folded his arms, holding her glance. He shook his head and sighed. "Such a woo-man. A woo-man of great power and beauty. Zee Goddess!"

"Yeah well, the Goddess is going to have the Sole Meunière, I think. What are you thinking about?"

He flashed a conspiratorial smile. "I don't dare tell you what I am sinking."

"I mean for food," she said, a little testier than she intended.

"Ah, zat."

She was not surprised when she finally heard his idea: a business proposal. He pulled bottles from his bag and set them on the table. Domaine Butschling's new line of less expensive Alsatian wines—a Riesling and a Pinot Blanc—under the label "Alsassy." He wanted Margot to do endorsements.

"I've got a pretty tight schedule these days, you know."

"But I knew you would 'elp out my family. You are part of zee family, Margot. And you 'ave expertise, great talent, and such beauty!"

"*Arret, toute cette merde.*"

"*Non, mais c'est vrai*! And you can make everyone

know the quality of zeez wines. Zat zey are complitly eunuch."

"Excuse me?"

"Zey 'ave no equal in zee world. Zey are extra spaycial!"

"Oh, you mean 'unique'! For a second there I thought you were breeding wine like cattle."

Fabrice laughed, tossed his blond hair, and finished his pitch in French. Embarrassment was not in his repertoire—something the League learned as we observed him over time.

We know that in the course of the lunch Margot agreed to do the endorsements. It certainly couldn't have been for the money; the Butschlings could not have afforded much. It might well have been because of her affection for Fabrice and his father. More likely, though, it was a result of her anger toward Brewster. It was no secret he disliked the Butschlings; all the more reason for her to help them now. Not exactly a revenge fuck, but a variation. Did she sleep with Fabrice, finally? It is very probable, though we will never know for certain. When asked about the subject by various tabloids and trade journalists, Fabrice flashed his mischievous smile and said, "No Comment," while Margot invariably said, "None of your damn business."

HOTTE MISERY

Brewster left the drawer open and the plastic container on his desk. His dull glance focused on the flashing red light of his answering machine. He punched the button. First was Mum, asking where he was and would he mind calling his mother if it wouldn't be too much trouble. Then his south of Market wine storage site, giving him their new hours for spring and summer. And then: the cold, choked anger of Margot's message.

It ranked among the worst moments of his life. Why hadn't he defused the situation long before? Why hadn't he distanced himself from his family and Isopropov? Why not just tell Margot the whole story? It was a case of alternating fear and optimism, he said. Fear that revealing the story would push Margot to reject him; optimism in telling himself his family story was a sideshow that wouldn't bother Margot at all. The combination was enough to keep him tragically silent.

He sat, head drooping, plunged into what he called "another entrails-to-jelly moment". It wasn't fair. It wasn't his fault he was part of the Hotte family. His parents were to blame. It could all be traced to their irresponsible sexual activity.

He called her, finally. It was by far their most explosive

face-off. They both seemed to know it wouldn't be enough to cause a permanent rupture, but they were badly bruised by it, nonetheless.

"You're not just snotty and detached and full of yourself, now you're a deceitful son of a bitch, too," she barked. "I'll bet you enjoyed your little secret, makin' an idiot out of me."

"This whole thing excruciating torture for me, Margot. I didn't know what to do. I didn't want to upset you, or risk losing you. This is—"

"So you thought I was yours to lose, is that it? Boy, you really are an egotistical bastard, aren't you?"

"That's not what I meant. I meant—I don't know—this doesn't seem like the moment to talk about how I feel about you, but—"

"Oh I know just how you feel about me. Somebody to manipulate and treat like shit. That's pretty much it."

"Look, I apologize, all right? I hate all this. Why don't we get together later, go to the Coup de Food and have some dinner. We can get this behind us."

"Easy for you to say! And quit your whining. I hate listenin' to that. I can't get together tonight, anyway; I'm meetin' somebody for dinner."

"Who?"

"None of your business. Fabrice Butschling."

"*What*? Seriously? What's he doing here?" Brewster's hand was so sweaty he could barely hold the receiver.

"What's anybody doin' anywhere?"

He was panicked. "You've got to be joking, Margot. That guy is a sleaze ball! You know that. He's *nul*, a *dragueur*, a hustler! He never met a mirror he didn't love.

112

He's so impressed with himself I can just…just see him leaning over the toilet bowl, admiring his turds."

"Oh Jesus, Brewster. You're losin' it. If you must know, I'm gonna do some endorsements for the Butschlings' new line of wines. Magazine and newspaper ads. I want to help 'em out."

Margot was not being truthful about the dinner, of course, but it had the desired effect on Brewster. He felt the blood drain from his head, and all the fight go out of him. He slipped into a warm bath of self-pity and finished the conversation in monosyllables. Bleak.

SPRING DINNER, 1991

Mum called to insist that he come for dinner. Though the background music was mercifully low, he could still make out the rubbery warbling of Dean Martin. Spring business meeting, she said. Friday.

"Sorry, Mum," he whispered. "I'm feeling pretty ill, nauseous and all. Can't do it."

"That's a shame, Nipper, but you'll have to manage somehow. This is *important*. Jock wants to talk about planning, and some guests are coming by beforehand—just for drinks—and your presence is required. You remember that very striking Russian woman, who works with Multishots? Nadia Scrotton or whatever? She'll be here; and Jock has invited the gentleman he just hired to supervise the sales division. Can't recall his name." Her voice shifted into an awkward sympathetic tone. Like talking to a puppy. "Nipper, why don't you try taking care of yourself? Fix yourself a few Isopropov-and-honey toddies. Get some rest. Four days should be plenty of time for you to recover, for heaven's sake. You're young...even if you're not in the best possible...shape." She sighed. "God knows, everything would be so much simpler if you had Bernadette to take care of you."

"Please don't start."

In the silence Brewster could hear her take a deep drag on her cigarette. "Fine. Be a drip. You don't have anything nice to say about the girl who woke up your winkie. Okay. But what about seeing my new wine cellar? It's so gorgeous. Aren't you even a little curious?"

"Of course. I can probably look at some wine bottles, if not drink any. "

"You'll be here, ready to enjoy Corinne's asparagus-anchovy bisque and hold up your end of the conversation. And that's that."

"At least if I puke on the table, people will just think I spilled some bisque."

"Nipper! Your prep-school mouth is not appreciated. We'll see you next Friday. Five sharp."

Brewster visited with Margot the night before the dinner, though she insisted he leave by eight, since she was going out. She would not say with whom. Their friendship saw them both determined to plow through the fog of bruised feelings that filled Margot's office as they sat and chatted. It was awkward, although less and less so as they drained the bottle of 1972 Gevrey-Chambertin from Ruineux that Brewster had brought along as a peace offering/ice breaker. He swore to her again that he had practically no involvement with Spodie International, that he never drank vodka—any vodka—-as she knew well. No talk of Fabrice Butschling, since Brewster's tentative question about him received only a dark look. When he left, he said he would see her at their Monday morning tasting.

As uncomfortable as it was, the visit settled his stomach and made the next few days more bearable for him, especially the dinner at Mum's, where for some reason

Jock's wife, Carolyn, seemed to compete with him for the Champagne consumption crown.

"I was very flattered, sure. Validation is so important in our lives!" said Carolyn, eyes wide, lashes working hard. Jock, Mum, Carolyn and Brewster sat in the parlor, chatting with Nadia, who looked restless and regal in her burgundy cowl-neck sweater and black three-quarter length skirt.

Jock broke in, turning toward Nadia. "You need to know that Carolyn works as Chief Astrologer for B of A here in the city—Did I mention that before? Anyway, she is so good at what she does—just like you are!—that she was just recently offered a great position with Wells. Very generous package, too, I might add," he said, beaming at Carolyn. "She might be willing to give you some astrology tips for your career. Wouldn't you, sweetie?"

"Oh, I'm sure Nadia is *so* successful that she doesn't need any help from the likes of me."

Looking coolly at Carolyn, Nadia spoke in a near-monotone. "I am certain you give valuable service to pipple, but I am not so interested in such service."

"Well, of course! Not everyone wants to work in harmony with the firmament." Carolyn gestured irritatedly with her champagne, splashing some on the huge Persian rug that covered most of the parlor floor.

"But sweetie, you've gotta tell everyone about the deal Wells was offering," Jock said quickly.

Carolyn shifted her gaze to Jock and her smile returned. "Yes, well. Such a surprise! But it was never going to happen. As I told Jock, their strategic planning is built around what they call their Necromancy Division—Tarot readers, psychics, clairvoyants—only about thirty percent are astrologers. Too eclectic, too decentralized for my taste. It makes it too hard to respond quickly to market dynamics. And I don't think I'd do well in close quarters with those other disciplines, anyway." She smiled ruefully. "The right money, but just totally the wrong vibe."

MR. BESTISH

A loose doorknob clacked, and Marvin Bestish padded into the parlor, escorted by Corinne. At fifty-one, Marvin was a fibrous, aging hippie, favoring paisley shirts under his safari jacket, and suede loafers for all occasions. He refused to give up his aviator glasses that carried a light blue tint. He had the right combination of world-weary charm and energy to be a national sales manager. An apologetic smile softened the effect of his small, reptilian eyes; his thinning hair, slicked straight back, nearly reached his shoulders. He inevitably brought with him a faint smell of good cigars. "Good evening, folks. Beautiful evening! Hope I'm not too late to enjoy one of the great Spodie International products?"

With a flourish, he kissed the hands of the ladies, starting with Mum, who blushed generously. He held Nadia's hand for a long moment. "Nice to see you, Nadia. Haven't seen you since Gorbachev was just a wee apparatchik." He shook Jock's hand, then Brewster's, turning quickly back to Jock.

"I'll have a tall glass of Bordelle, if you please. Or wait! How about one of those fantastic new Butschling wines, maybe an Alsassy Pinot Blanc? With a touch of soda?"

Brewster nearly choked on his champagne. "Uh, sorry, what? What was that?"

Jock held up an open palm. "Hold it, *basta*. I—"

Marvin broke in. "I get it. You object. Club soda in a product like this, even a small amount, well, the Butschlings might not approve right away. But let me ask you all: why would you be a purist when you're limiting options for serving the product? Enjoy these treasures straight up, with dinner? Sure. But in my book any time is right for this kind of super hip, top flight product."

"Right, right, right," Jock said hurriedly. "And well said, Marv. It's just that we're jumping the gun a little bit here. I hadn't gotten around to letting the family in on the latest exciting portfolio additions."

"Oh boy, I put my foot on a turd, didn't I?" Then, shifting gears to mischievous: "But you can't blame me for getting excited about great product."

"So the company is handling the cheap Butschling stuff?" said Brewster. "And this just happened?"

Jock smiled testily at Brewster. "Nipper, this was part of the reason for this get-together. Now just fasten your seat belt and you'll get all the information."

"So it's a done deal?"

"It certainly is. Which is plenty of reason for you to get off my case. *Now*." He turned to Corinne, who stood by the door. "Corinne, would you please get Mister Bestish his drink?"

Uncomfortable silence. The clinking of glassware and bottles at the wet bar.

"Well, isn't this *fun*!" said Mum. "And so nice to meet you, Mister Bestish. I have to say, Jackson hasn't filled us in on your background, so maybe you could tell us something about yourself. You must be quite the expert in wine and spirits."

Bestish chuckled drily, then cleared his throat. "Nah. Not at all! My dear Missus Hotte, the fact is, I don't know jack. I'm too lazy! I'm happier just showing products to all those expert tasters out there—and they're all experts, you know." He winked. "I let 'em tell me what *they* think. It gives 'em a chance to educate the unwashed."

"But keep in mind, Mum, Marv had some of the best sales numbers in the history of Crudrunners, the big Chicago distributor," Jock added quickly. "I don't think I'm pushing the thing too hard, Marv, to call you one of the country's top guys."

"Thanks, but I'm sticking to my story: I'm no big-shot expert. I just show customers good products and they buy 'em. If they need a little push, I pull out a review from the *Intoxicator*, or whatever. Great stuff like this," he said, holding up the tumbler Corinne had just given him, "sells itself."

"Well, since you're too modest, I can toot your horn a little," said Jock. "Anybody ever heard of Baron Phil's Wide-Mouth Bordeaux?"

Mum said, "Did you do that one, Mr. Bestish? That's a very big seller, isn't it?"

"Huge," said Jock.

"Well now, I didn't make the wine or anything. But I did come up with a pretty sweet idea. It was a night when I was just sitting around drinking, you know? So as I pour another glass of whatever the hell I was having, I say to myself, 'Why is this opening so small? It's taking forever to get this stuff into the glass, where I can get at it! I was just impatient to get at all that culture, you know? So I threw a hexagram, and I got 'Early Good Fortune—Pizza Toppings Give Pleasure.' I saw that as a clear green light. And that's how Wide Mouth Bordeaux was born."

"What was that you said about hexes?" Mum asked.

"Oh, sorry about that, Missus Hotte. I keep thinking everybody does yoga and Tai Chi these days. Hexagrams are part of the I-Ching, a totally right-on, ancient Chinese book of wisdom. I've been seriously into it for many years. I highly recommend it to anybody who is facing heavy decisions, or who just wants to keep his head straight."

"So Baron Phil's came out of an I-Ching reading?" said Jock.

"Scout's honor," said Marv, raising his hand. "Once I got into gear, it all fell into place. I got a custom bottle mold made, with a neck twice as wide. Bingo."

"Is it good wine?" said Carolyn, looking a little troubled at talk of the I-Ching, which she had no use for.

"It's great! Nothing wrong with it. With a great concept, great packaging, I told the Baron Phil people that most of their work was done for 'em. They just needed some value-added water in the bottle to make it all happen. That's what I call wine in this price range—value-added water."

"Whatever you're doing, Marv, it's magic. Pure magic. And I say just keep on keepin' on! So! Why don't we talk about our new products, since we're already on the topic?" He slid to the edge of his wing chair, his eyes glowing. "Prepare to be blown away. First, two of the three additions to our list are high-end products, which means enhanced company image in the industry and in the public view, too.

That is *major*. Second, these are both high-margin products. So we're not giving up anything to run with the big cats. By next Christmas, I'm telling you, we are going to see numbers the baby Jesus himself would go nuts for.

"So let me scope all this out for you. First, we're positioning ourselves to blow a huge hole in the seven to ten dollar Chardonnay market with 'California Chardonnastic.' Spodie International'll be the first on the planet to offer what I'm calling a 'Chardonnay drink'! And I promise you, it's gonna be *major*! We're talking prestige label design, with a big gold medallion at the lower left, something like 'Now! With ten percent real Chardonnay!' I got Fective Global Flavor Labs in New Jersey working right now putting finishing touches of the recipe, and we're green-lighted to put 'All Natural Ingredients' on the label."

"Like I told you, Jock: sheer genius. I'm in love," muttered Marvin.

Brewster downed the last of his champagne. "Can I just ask? What's the other ninety percent going to be? If ten percent is Chardonnay?"

"Relax, Nipper. This is why God made water. And carrageenan, and citric acid, and natural flavors. When you taste it in a couple of weeks, you'll feel better. Also, as you just heard, we've secured west coast distribution of the new lower-tier Alsatian wines from Domaine Butschling, in Colmar, France. You'll really love this deal, Mum, because along with it comes a limited number of cases of their high-end wines. All the—"

"I think we're all going to take it in the high end," said Brewster, louder than he intended.

"You're out of order, Nipper," Jock snapped. "Why

don't you get yourself some more champagne?" He cleared his throat and tossed a meaningful look at Mum. "As I was saying, the different vineyard names and all that are too much of a mouthful for me, but these things are *big* out there in the wine world."

"That sounds lovely. So I'll get some for my new cellar?"

"Absolutely. Whatever you want, Mum. Now, cases are limited to begin with, but the Butschlings have promised to ramp us up year by year. So. What do you say we focus on our last addition, a real blockbuster. This is one everybody's gonna love. So exciting! We're going to market an ultra-premium version of Isopropov! And we're calling it—are you ready?—Isopropov Silver Tinkle."

Bestish and Brewster both began talking; Brewster stopped, gesturing in deference.

"You got volume and margins on this?" asked Bestish.

"Let me finish, Marv. I want you all to know that this isn't some average gut-ruster vodka. It's ground-breaking, original stuff, different from anything out there now. And where are we gonna sell it? Now get this—I can hardly stand it—we're not just talking domestic broad market, we want to see European distribution, east *and* west, if things pan out in the reshuffle of the Warsaw Pact countries. Plus great placements in Russia itself! Like the Citizen Comrade Luxury Boutique chain, no less. That's how special it is. That's why we're gonna kick the butts of Blottoskaya and Insolent and all the others. We're looking at a launch this fall. And I want to give you all the chance to personally thank Nadia for the great global marketing effort Multishots has pledged to the product." His applause prompted the others to join in, though Brewster's was slow and ironic.

Nadia's mouth twitched a tiny smile. "Thank you. Multishots is heppy to be part of this, and to work with Hotte family—and Mister Bestish—is great pleasure and privilege. I am sure you will be plizzed with campaign we designed." She lifted her champagne flute. "*Zhelayu, chtoby vse,*" she said, meeting Jock's eye.

"What does that mean?" asked Mum.

"It mins we celebrate." Her eyes met Jock's again. "And it mins 'can you get younger brother to conwince that woman Margot Sipski to shut her mouth about wodka?'"

"Now Nadia, that's not really a topic for this moment. I told you I'd have a word with my brother when the time was right."

"Soonest is best," said Nadia, standing up. "I must go. Thank you for champagne, was delicious." To Marvin: "We should meet with your boss to talk about sales plan."

Marvin stood. "Hey, I know you gotta run, Nadia, but I was hoping you could give us some inside dope on what's happening in Mother Russia. Pretty confusing since the wall went down and all those little republics seem like they want to take their balls and go home. So to speak. Can't you tell us something?"

"No reason to be too worried for our project. It is mess in Soviet Union now, true, but Russia will have success with new chairman of Russian Republic, Yeltsin. Russia has no need for bunch of loser Asian republics like Azerbaijan. They drink only little, anyway. Gorbachev is not to be powerful much longer, Yeltsin is main man. It will all be fine, and you will sell lots of wodka." She smiled lazily. "Goodbye, all. *Paka!*"

Primp Magazine — April 1991

ONE-ON-ONE WITH: MARGOT SIPSKI

Everywhere you look these days, people are talking about success. But who are the people who live it? The ones who are independent enough to care about it, even? The ones who are bolder, sassier, sexier—just like you want your hair to be? One answer to that question comes in the imposing form of Margot Sipski, the 33-year-old wine-tasting whiz who has taken California and the whole country by storm. After tasting her way to fame and fortune in France—the ooh-la-la capital of wine—she has returned and re-tuned to California as a way of life. Currently doing exclusive (and pricey!) private tastings for aficionados in San Francisco, she is also fielding a strong anti-vodka campaign as well as managing a roster of product endorsements that would make the most driven sports legend or movie star go grapevine green with envy. Margot lets her long, casually asymmetrical hair down for us here, with some candid comments on hot topics. She's a special vintage!

ON HER BEGINNINGS: *"I was born in a crossfire hurricane. Oh wait, was that Mick Jagger? I get us mixed up. I'm from Fresno, California—an actual crossfire hurricane, but with really heavy fog during the winter."*

ON THE VALUE OF FAILURE: "Unless it's covered by your insurance or gets you a nice consolation prize, I say stay away from it."

ON FRANCE: "God's country and God's people. I'd wear a beret if it didn't look so damn military on me."

ON CALIFORNIA: "As long as you stay close to the coast, you can hardly beat it."

ON WINE: "Beyond the poseurs and snotty people, it's way beautiful. But remember to brush your teeth. That sh** will ruin 'em if you're not careful."

ON SUCCESS: "I totally fell into it; but if anyone asks, I tell 'em I'm a genius."

ON MAKEUP: "If my eyelids are weighed down a little, I know I've got it right."

ON LOVE: "Do something that makes you honestly happy—not something that just makes you breathe hard."

ON FASHION: "As long as I'm not getting arrested for indecent exposure, I'm fine."

ON VODKA: "I know a scam when I taste one."

THE BORSCHT THICKENS

That spring seemed interminable, slower than a bad bartender. It was windy and cool in the city, and Brewster was depressed. He had no contact with anyone from the League. He was trying to finish a long feature article for *The National Intoxicator* about the wine cellars of America's greatest Washington lobbyists, but it was hard to focus. He still managed to have dinner with Margot twice a week and force himself to taste wine with her on Monday and Wednesday mornings, but it was leaden, joyless. Unmoored from the League even temporarily he was a lost soul, and it was torture to be with Margot and not unburden himself about his suspension.

"You're gonna have to come clean, Brewster," she said one day after a tasting. "I can tell you've got something going on. Are you still pissed off at me for kickin' your ass about your daddy's vodka? Is that it? That was months ago."

"No, no, really. I'm fine. Just haven't been feeling well."

"That's bullshit. You think I'm blind?" She paused, her face softening. "Brewster, I'm your friend, remember? You're always lookin' out for me; well, I'm lookin' out for you, too. You've got a rooster inside you, and he's got to crow eventually, I can tell you."

"Okay. Okay, fine." He was thinking fast. "I might as well get it off my chest. I've been feeling bad about hiding the truth about the company, you're right. But you can't blame me for not liking Fabrice Butschling hanging around, either. The guy's just plain sleazy. He's a *gugusse*."

She sighed. "You gotta get off that. Mostly you need to get two messages from me. One, I think you're one amazin' guy; and two, I don't belong to you, or anyone—including Fabrice. I'm into wine, remember? I told you that when we met at that weird tasting in Burgundy. You gotta get outta your fantasy world."

"That's just what Bernadette would say." To nudge the discussion elsewhere, he said, "I'm unhappy about being such a spineless bastard, too. It's always the same old story with me and great wines. Put 'em in front of me and I'm done, no sense of proportion, no restraint. It's worse than embarrassing. You know, a few months ago I was in LA. at a tasting where they had great old vintages of Montrachet—and I just lost it. There were '61s and '62s that were so beautiful—kind of somber and without lots of fruit, but so rich and full and subtle. Kind of stately, really—all that great sort of bacon and pork fat stuff, lots of cognac spice and creamy butterscotch. And crazy palate coverage, especially the 61s."

"Did you taste the Lafoney '61? That was spectacular."

"Thanks for using the word 'taste.' 'Guzzled' was more like it. But yeah, I did. That, and the Marquis de Pastiche. But I really couldn't hold back with the '77s and '78s, either. I made a total pig of myself. A puking pig, of course." He looked rueful. "I was helpless. It's sad."

She nodded matter-of-factly. "Yup. It is."

"I'm just an alcoholic."

"But a real picky one. There's that."

At the end of June came the late-night gunshot through a window of Margot's office. She called him around 3:30 a.m., trying to make light of it. He could hear the sound of voices in the background, the crackle of police radios. "Are you all right? Are you hurt?" he said.

"I'm okay. Really. The front window doesn't looks so good, though. Is this comin' out of my security deposit?"

"That isn't a bit funny, Margot. I'll be right over." He threw on some clothes and covered the distance to her place at a dead run. She met him at the door, got him past the yellow crime scene tape, introduced him to a couple of policemen who had already questioned her. When they asked him if he had any idea who might do such a thing, he was caught off guard and said no. Only later, when he talked to Margot alone, did she tell him she had mentioned to the police her anti-vodka campaign as a possible factor, but told them she had no idea about the actual shooter.

The next day, more disturbing news. He learned in a phone conversation with Mum that Jock was making an unusually large number of trips to Moscow. The few details she gave him were odd. First, he'd gone to Moscow the previous December. He'd never done that. And he had returned five times since, never with Carolyn. Normal yearly travel to Russia for Jock would have been, say, two trips: the Univod Producers Convention in June, with Carolyn in tow; maybe putting in an appearance at the UNESCO World Ethanol Day in September, or at the International Drinkers for Jesus festival in St. Petersburg. But five trips, all in the last six months? It was mystifying.

He called the Bat, told her about the shooting and about Jock's travels. And it was suddenly relevant to tell her about Nadia Scrotova's comment about Margot at the meeting at Mum's place. He even mentioned the development of the upscale vodka product, though he doubted even that could account for so much travel.

"So I need you to find out what my brother's up to. Did he travel alone on those trips? It would be good to know what Nadia is up to, too. Maybe there's some screwing going on the side? God, that'll make things extra messy."

The Bat stopped chewing and shifted her bubblegum into her cheek. "Personally, I like the sexy jobs, but okay, I think I got it. You want info about your brother's plane trips and about the Russky chic. And you want to know if he's fuckin' her. Right?"

"Not necessarily in that order, but yeah, that'll do. Sooner the better."

"You got it, Toyota. But I was gonna say, why don't you let me keep an eye on Our Lady of the Eyeliner for a while, too? I can do a better job than some dumbass security service with those little dipshit window sensors."

"You can't do all this by yourself, can you?"

"I told you before, Brew, I got lots of friends in low places. They work hard and they work, uh, real discreet. And cheap. So don't worry, I'm gonna do my usual kick-ass job. What you gotta do is take me over there to meet Missus Zorro, so she knows who I am and what the plan is."

"And what is the plan?"

"For her place, twenty-four hour surveillance for three weeks, and then we'll see where we get. I'm gonna do one shift myself."

"That's a lot of work."

"Don't worry, you're payin' me, remember?"

They met at Margot's office that afternoon. There were wary introductions.

"So you're gonna be hangin' around outside, waiting for somethin' to happen? Seems like that juice ain't worth the squeezin'," said Margot.

"Don't worry about it, Mizz Sipski. Like I told Brew: I got lots of friends who are good at this stuff. You won't even know we're around. But you need to know it's happening, is all. I'm gonna give you my card in case somethin' comes up and you can't get a hold of Brew." She rummaged around in her huge, worn leather bag with buckskin fringe, slung over her shoulder. "Here ya go. Anybody want a Double Bubble? I'm ready for a fresh one," she said, spitting the old wad into the new wrapper and tossing it into the basket next to Margot's desk.

Brewster rolled his eyes. "No. Thanks. And by the way, as the landlord I'm having bulletproof glass put in all these windows. I've got to protect my investment," he said, eyeing Margot severely. "And to be safe, I bought you one of these new wireless cell phones," he said, pulling a slab of gray plastic out of the shopping bag he was carrying. "I got one for myself, too, and they're both activated as of this morning. You should give your number to Heidi and nobody else. Take it with you wherever you go. The number taped on the back is mine. You have to promise to call if you notice anything even a little unusual. Right?"

She shook her head. "You're nuts, but you're the boss. Arguin' with you is like a bug arguin' with a chicken."

A FRENCH CROCODILE DUNDEE

Less than a week later, the Bat was back in Brewster's office. She sat in her spot next to his desk, squirming in the chair. "Swear to God, I hate these yoga pants. Got 'em on sale at Penny's. They chafe like a mother, especially at Taekwondo. Makes me nuts." She looked around innocently. "So what are we drinkin'?"

Brewster was impatient, knowing she had news about Jock and Nadia. But he would play it her way. "This is an excellent Chinon, a '76 from Bernard Drouly. Get yourself a glass."

"Thought you'd never ask."

"And get rid of your gum."

"Okay, *okay.*"

"So are you going to tell me what you've got, or what?"

The Bat was pouring herself a big glass, leaning over and eyeing the fill height. "Hey, I'm concentrating here, I'll be right with ya."

"You know very well you shouldn't be pouring that so full. You can't swirl it that way."

"To each his own, Brew. Back in Jersey, we like to have a good blast of whatever we're drinkin' before we start thinkin' about the smell."

He sighed. "Whatever. So shall we talk?"

She sat again, took an audible swallow and perched her glass on the edge of the desk. "Tasty, but kind of light, don't ya think? I mean, where's the beef?"

"Heidi."

"Okay, okay. Lemme lay it out for ya. I hadda do some research on the side to figure this one out, but I got you some serious goodies. You're gonna brown your brockies." She pulled three photos out of a manila envelope and slid them onto Brewster's desk.

"Holy shit," he whispered. The first photo showed Fabrice Butschling and Nadia coming out of the Multishots offices on Pine Street. The other two were grainy, low-light pictures of them sitting very close, having dinner in an Asian restaurant.

"Holy shit is right! Am I the pooch's nuts, or what? I had to dig down pretty deep to find out about this guy, but you know him, right? He collected cash from the eyeliner queen. So he flies out here, but he ends up hanging out with Boy-tits. They went to a place all the way out in the Sunset, figuring nobody'd recognize 'em. Hah. The guy kinda looks like Crocodile Dundee, doesn't he—I mean if ya don't count the long hair. Anyway, he's a nimrod. Didn't even know how to order Thai. Not sure if he's bonin' her or not, but that info's comin' soon."

Brewster shook his head in wonder. "But what's it about? What are they up to?"

"Can't say yet, but I'm on it, no sweat. I just hadda give you the fresh info, since you were so hot about the whole thing. And, AND, I got another bomb for ya. You'll love it."

"Seriously?"

"I would not shit ya," she said, pulling a sheaf of papers out of the same envelope. "Check out the flight manifests."

"Amazing," said Brewster, scanning the sheets quickly. "She went on every trip with him."

"You got it. But check out the destinations. Three of those flights are to Riga. That's in Latvia."

"Thank you."

She grunted. "Latvia. Makes East Jesus look like Paris. When I was a kid, I thought Latvia was some kinda pancake."

"So how long until we get more information on all this stuff?"

She took another swallow of wine. "You know how this works. I just dunno. Bet it'll be less than a week, though."

"So how is the surveillance of Margot's place going?"

"Pretty quiet. She's like a nun, your friend. Only goes out for shopping and those tastings and stuff she does. Sometimes she has a coffee with some dikey-lookin' buddies, winemakers, I think. That's kinda it. Any way you can talk her out of doin' her public tastings for a couple of months? They're ruinin' my Arid Extra Dry. Just this last Tuesday, she did one at Fort Punter, musta been four hundred people. No way to control that space, for sure."

"I'll talk to her about it."

The Bat flashed a grim smile. "Maybe I should talk to her. Seems like your credibility is in the crapper."

PRESTIGIOUS DIRT

A cross town that same afternoon, there was a meeting at Jock's office. Fabrice, Nadia, and Jock lounged on a sleek, spare sectional at one end of the room, while Marvin stood facing them. Snifters on the thick glass coffee table, splashy rented abstract art on the walls.

Marvin was excited. "It's a hell of a campaign, ready to go, Fabrice. The stuff's gonna sail off the shelf. I got solid commitments from west coast distributors to take everything you've got, right now. I got a full on-sale program, with a dozen new drink recipes for bartenders—great ones like the 'Quiche Me,' made with cream and bacon-flavored Isopropov—as a nice tie-in—and the 'Strasbourg Goose,' with grenadine and goose liver bitters. They'll break down the doors to get this stuff."

"So eet eez no problem zat we 'ave not enough grapes from our vineyards to make volumes we need?"

"Nah! Don't worry about that. It's a detail." Marvin waved off the question like a pesky insect.

Jock looked earnest. "Fabrice. You need to let us steer this thing. You go on making your gorgeous boutique bottlings and we'll take care of the Alsassy brand. The truth is, we've researched this thoroughly and feel confident that we can supply enough product to fulfill our most aggressive projections, and without compromising the quality that your brand name demands. That's a promise from me to you."

"But eef zee label says zee wine eez not from our estate?"

Jock's face glowed with evangelical fervor. "It won't even have to be from your *region*! Fabrice, nobody reads the fine print on labels. Nobody'll *care*. Once they experience such mind-bending, fabulous flavor, they'd buy it if it came from the moon!" He cleared his throat. "Now, we also need to talk about ads and promotion. Nadia, as you know, is working with us on the side to get things going in Russia, and those are connections you just can't buy. Marv, you got more for Fabrice on the domestic market?"

"Right. I'm not gonna sugar-coat this, Fabrice. You're going to have to put some shoe leather into this project. I'm putting together a twenty-city tour that'll be at gonzo speed. What I'll need for you to do is pack light—no suits, nothing fancy. We need shirts that show chest hair—you got chest hair, right? And jeans or some kind of French work pants, nice and worn, but clean—they gotta be clean. We want you out there as Alsace's version of Nature Boy. You've got the rugged good looks; we just need to punch 'em up." Reaching into his brief case he said, "I also have a couple of these that will come in handy."

Fabrice looked confused. "What eez zat?"

Marvin laughed. "What'd ya mean? It's a glass jar. Full of soil from your vineyards!"

"But 'ow did you get eet?"

He laughed again, harder. "Come on, get hip, Fabrice.

It's not the real stuff. Why bother with all that? I scooped this up from the landscaping out front of Jock's house. Tossed in a little handful of gravel from the walkway. Lookin' good, huh? Listen, buyers eat this stuff up. You take the lid off, let 'em touch some real dirt! Let 'em *smell* it! Tell 'em it's the secret behind all your great wines. They'll pee their pants!"

Jock cleared his throat. "So, Fabrice. Along with all that, we're still counting on you to get Margot Sipski to do national print and local broadcast for us. That's still doable, right?"

"Honestly, I sink she eez not excited since she finds out about you being zee distributor. A big problem is your brozair. He tells her not to do eet."

Jock looked grim. "I should have known Brewster would stick his nose in this."

"You must do something about that little shit, Jock. Brother or not," said Nadia. "If you don't—"

"Relax, Nadia. I'll work it out with him. He responds to pressure, thank God. So, with Brewster not voicing an opinion on it, you think she'll do it?"

Fabrice gave a little shrug. "I sink so. Eet might take a leetle time."

Jock and Marvin exchanged glances. " Marv?"

"Yeah, fine. As long as we get her to sign contracts by mid-next week. She's still doing all this gratis?"

"I sink so, but I weel find zat out as well. Margot and I are old, spaycial friends, you know."

"Sure, great. Now, I hope you'll excuse us. We've got some other company business on the calendar, and time is always so short."

Fabrice got to his feet. "No problem. Sank you ole for your time." He glanced questioningly at Nadia.

"I will come to see you at seven?" she said.

"*Parfait, chérie.*" He smiled, relieved.

When he was gone, Jock got to his feet and went over to his desk. "Gotta have something to eat. Low blood sugar." He opened a drawer and pulled out a cellophane bag. "Anybody want some Cheezows? Love these things," he muttered, ripping the bag with his teeth.

"Not any for me, pliz," said Nadia, looking impatient.

"God, I'd love some, Jock, but I always get that yellow shit all over myself," said Marvin.

"More for me then," he said, jamming some puffs into his mouth. "Mmmm. I usually juft—just eat this stuff to piss off snotty goons like my brother, if I know they're gonna to be around." He sat, tossing the bag on the coffee table. "Okay, so it looks like Fabrice is giving us a green light on control of production, which is great. Once we get rolling, I'll bet the gradual phase out of grapes won't get a peep out of him. I'm a little worried, honestly though, about him finding out about Global Ersatz and the flavor augmentation. Once most of the actual wine is out of the products, he might get grumpy."

Marvin looked skeptical. "I think it's all a go. I threw a hexagram early this morning and got "Wisdom is Practical—Nurses in the Smoking Section." That's super positive. But we'll have to stroke him for a few months after he signs and finds out the real story. I don't even think he's checked in with his dad about the deal."

"I hev to say to you both, I think you are poosies," said Nadia, leaning back into the sofa., exasperated. "Why are you so worried? If I hev learned anything about this guy, is that cash matters most. Marvin, once you have numbers on new bigger margins, how will anyone not like this deal? His father will agree while he masturbates himself." She gave Marvin a regal glance. "Since you are standing. It is empty, my glass."

"More wine?"

Nadia sneered. "You are kidding me? French boy is gone. Wodka!"

Marvin smiled. "Okay, sure. Which blend?"

"Hundred fifty proof. Pliz."

"They're still in the freezer?" Marvin asked Jock. He nodded, and Marvin opened the freezer compartment of the rosewood-finished fridge that stood against the wall opposite the sectional. "We still agree the hundred proof will be the final version for the market, though, right?"

"Absolutely," said Jock. "It's the most commercial, but still kicks the shit out of you."

"As I said, you are both poosies," muttered Nadia, knocking back her drink.

"That's my cuddly Nadia," said Jock. "Just don't get too fond of French cooking."

Nadia gave a disgusted grunt. "You are always jealous, you playboy. Just because your wife chirps like bird and has sand in her loins."

"Nadia, you are such a rude bitch."

"Is why you love me."

Marvin cleared his throat. "So, what if Sipski won't sign on for the Butschling marketing?" said Marvin.

"I don't see that as a big deal, honestly," said Jock, still annoyed. He leaned back, stretching out his legs. "We can find a great plan B without much hassle. Maybe we get Julia Child."

Marvin snorted. "You want an old lady selling the wines? Not that she'd do it."

"Okay, maybe we get a TV star—maybe Hasselhoff, or Tom Selleck." He chuckled. "Maybe we get Farrah Fawcett to shoplift a bottle, I dunno."

"Jock. You got any idea how much they'd want? You've got a big budget for this? I mean a *really* big budget? It would be best if Sipski did it. She's got the tasting chops and a super profile. And she's cheap."

"Is just what I think of her. A cheap fuck," said Nadia.

"You know what you should do, Marv. Check in with one of those idiot British wine societies and see if there isn't some upper class twit with a little name recognition who could be our Plan B. You know, one of those guys with a posh accent and big brown teeth."

Marvin agreed it was a good idea. Jock said he had some details on the European launch of Silver Tinkle to work out with Nadia, and gently invited him to leave. Which was when Jock and Nadia got down to even more serious business. The plan to kidnap Margot.

A PLOT, AMONG OTHERS

Jock sat close to Nadia, thigh to thigh. He kissed the back of her neck. "God! I could hardly keep my hands off you. It was torture!"

"You have no discipline," she said, pulling away.

"That's right, blame the victim." He poured more Silver Tinkle for both of them and they began discussing the Plan. It was a plan so far-reaching and audacious in its scope that even our best League analyst had no clue about it until the denouement, which was just days away at that point.

"You know, this stuff is pretty good with Cheezows, I gotta say. Maybe we can get a tie-in with those guys. Sure you don't want some?" He slid the bag in her direction.

Nadia flashed him a dark look. "So, situation is fluid right now. Delicate. We maintain control of Yeltsin, and Univod is happy to support him at this moment. He is clear about obligations to us directly. We keep him in good supply of hundred proof version, there is no reason we cannot control him and Univod completely." She plinked the snifter with her long scarlet nails.

"Right, it's gotta be the hundred proof," said Jock. "He's not gonna be functional if he gets into the one-fifty. The guy amazes me, able to drink so much and still do his presidential duties, or whatever." He snuffled a laugh. "Your guys feel sure about his brand loyalty, right?"

'Of course. And if saying this you are fishing for compliment, I am happy to give it. It is very, very special wodka, Jockushka. You are genius."

Jock grinned. "Yeah. Yeah, I s'pose so. I can't let you forget what a hard time you gave me about getting research funds to Blacktech." He poured the last Cheezow crumbs into his palm and tossed them into his mouth.

"You were not the one performing off-record negotiation with Latvia."

"Okay, I wasn't. But I told you they'd fall all over themselves for hard currency. A little gene splicing? What do they care? They would've let us use their plow horses to make party dip if we'd asked. So. What about the raw materials issue? Are we good to go with expanded wheat acreage?"

"All will be near Smolensk. A little more than two thousand new hectares."

"Ass-kicking! You are the *best*, sweetheart! And that's confirmed?"

"It is. Yeltsin is huge help, and is horse to bet on, but Natasha tells that it is hard to manage his drink. She keeps him in what she calls 'sweet spot'—barely drunk, but not more."

"Well you tell that girl we love her over here. Can't you guys get her a promotion, or more money or something?"

"She collects already a salary as president's personal aide, and also much money from Univod. No worry for her. A good worker, loyal to us, not to Univod." She took a swallow of vodka. "We must have conversation about that Sipski bitch."

"True. And I've got the solution to that little issue. But first you've got to stop getting me all worked up." He took her hand and put it on his crotch. "It's all your fault."

Nadia left her hand there for a moment. She grazed the bulging zipper with her nails, fixing him with a cool stare. "We have not time, and you know this." Her eyes narrowed. "I have solution for the problem, too. We kill her now. I personally will put my fist through bridge of her nose."

"Baby, no! No, that's all wrong, can't you see that? You do that and everyone's gonna suspect Big Vodka. They'll come after you, you'll be under the microscope. I've got a much better idea."

"But we can make car accident or something."

"Nope. Here's what we do. We kidnap her."

"Kidnap her why? So we can kill her after?"

He gave her a cagey glance. "Come on, babe, you're smarter than that. Look, we kidnap her, all right? We take her to one of the warehouses in South City. We don't identify ourselves, but we put out word that she can be ransomed for—I don't know—say ten million dollars. Money to be deposited into a blind Swiss account. And *then* what do we do?"

"Torture her?"

"No! Univod puts up the ransom money. Very publicly! They do it because even if they obviously disagree with Sipski about vodka's value and its place in the world, they realize that she's a valuable and talented member of the wine and spirits community, and they think the world'd be a less interesting place without her, blah—blah—blah, whatever. But the effect is perfect. Suddenly she's de-fanged. How can she keep screaming about vodka when vodka rescued her ass? Huh? If she does, she looks like the worst kind of ingrate. It'll kill her reputation." He leaned back and crossed his arms. "And how is she gonna refuse to do the ads for the Butschling products after that, huh? Margot Sipski neutralized—better than murder!"

"And who are the kidnappers?"

"I'm counting on you to figure that out. Whatever you do, don't use any of those east-coast thugs from Brighton Beach. Way too obvious. Find some Algerians or something, some people who don't like France. That's a good angle. Let me know what you come up with. The other great asset we've got is Fabrice."

Nadia nodded. "To help catch her. Of course. Good."

"So you tell him you really admire Sipski, it's a girl thing. Two strong women in the business world, that sort of shit. You want to meet with her to bury the hatchet. There's a ton of endorsement work that you'd like to throw her way—not vodka, of course, but other products—brandies, liqueurs, lots of stuff. You tell him he needs to set up a meeting of just the three of you, to hear the possibilities. It's all for Sipski's benefit! But you gotta tell him he can't identify you when he talks to her, otherwise she won't show up. He has to tell her the meeting is with a major industry figure who wants to help her. But you tell *him* you just want a chance to get straight with her."

"So we must have muscle to take her quickly." She nodded absently, visualizing the scenario. "It will be in parking lot of south of Market restaurant, maybe. Spoon Goon. Maybe Gravy Stain."

"Just where I was headed. We need an isolated spot, but nothing that makes her suspicious. Isn't The Gravy Stain on 13th, around Sykoe Avenue? That's perfect. It's like a junkyard down there, but I saw they just got a nice review in The Bay Gawk."

"Is good idea. Not too much light there."

"Right. So it's up to you to convince Fabrice to sell her the idea. Use your magic."

"I am not complaining, but there is limit to what I can do. He stinks. And is terrible lover."

He laughed, leaned over and kissed her. "Babe, I love hearing you say that, but—"

"Because he is worse than you, even?" She gave him a cool, challenging smile.

"I'm one of those rare secure males, sweetie, so don't even start with that shit. And don't tell me your problems. I don't care if he needs mirrors and Barry White tapes and you in a nurse's outfit. You've gotta do this. The whole plan depends on it."

"I know what to do. I ask him to pick me up, bring me to restaurant. Like that, we have her arrive alone. I can stall few minutes at my office so Fabrice and I arrive after the bitch is taken and gone."

"Great, good. No need to get lover boy involved more than he needs to be. It could be a health hazard for him."

She grunted. "It will be fine. He has not the brain to suspect me. Now what about idiot boy, your brother? She will tell him about this, certainly, and he will come to you, asking questions."

"I thought of that. You let me worry about Brewster. You just need to line up the muscle for the job and keep Fabrice on the hook. This thing is about timing. It's all gonna be about timing."

145

THE BAT CONNECTS THE DOTS

Brewster buzzed the Bat into the office. She was breathless. "Jesus, Brew, I got pretty wild stuff here. I'm skippin' my master class for this, so you owe me big." She tossed a manila envelope on the desk, and sat. "There's still lotsa holes in the story, but you're gonna want to put me in your will, I swear." She smiled wryly. "And no kissin' on the mouth, 'kay?" Gesturing at the envelope, she said, "First of all, and before we even mention the story about Missus Zorro, did you know your brother's mixed up in big time Russian politics? Hah?"

"*What?*"

"Good answer. That was my first choice, too, when my wiretap guys dumped this shit on me. But it's all there," she said, reaching over and yanking a stack of papers from the envelope. "Fifty-some pages of transcript, bub, some calls from your brother to Miss Boy-tits, some to a coupla dipshits named Alexei and Maxim, in Moscow, at a brand new Univod department, the Ministry of Mail Order Brides. Not sure what that's about. Their English is so shitty it was hard to make 'em out, but one thing's sure: they're doin' more than just makin' vodka. These guys are handlers of the new big cheese in Russia, that guy Yeltsin. It's especially weird because these numbnuts weren't even on a secure line! I mean, you gotta be fuckin' kiddin'."

Brewster stared at her for moment. "I need a drink," he said. "What the hell is happening?" He crossed the room and began rummaging through his small cooler unit.

"Honest to God, it's weird, Brew. But lemme tell you the deal." She craned her neck in his direction. "You're gettin' me a glass, right?"

Brewster straightened up, inspecting the label of a bottle. "Yeah, of course. Just as soon as you get rid of your gum."

"I was gettin' to that, don't worry. Christ, you're picky."

He uncorked the bottle and returned to the desk looking grim, holding two half-full glasses. "1970 Chateau Rieustat-Spleen, from Saint Julien. It needs to warm up a little. Better than either of us deserves."

"Hey, speak for yourself. And this is kind of a chintzy pour, isn't it?"

"Please—just tell me what you know," said Brewster, looking pained.

"Well, it's pretty spotty, like I say. But the deal is that Boy-tits and your asshole brother are workin' with Tweedle Dum and Tweedle Dee at the Kremlin there, to kinda manage Yeltsin. The real pisser is, I dunno exactly what they want from him yet. But we'll get it. The weird part is, it looks like Yeltsin is absolutely fuckin' in love with that new vodka you guys got—whadya callit?"

"Silver Tinkle."

"Yeah, that's what I said. Lemme show you the place in the transcript where…" She flipped through some pages, scattering them on the desk. "…here ya go. This is only a week ago. Check it out. The only call we got where Yeltsin is right there in the room, gettin' translated by the borscht brothers."

JACKSON: You have to tell the president how thrilled we are that he's enjoying Silver Tinkle. We're just so excited.

MAXIM: (unintelligible exchange) He says not to worry about thrills and excitement. Just send more cases, direct to us. Maybe forty?

JACKSON: The last fifteen are gone? Already?

MAXIM: Yes, is true. You know, lots of entertaining, cocktails, receptions. And how do you say, pilfering?

JACKSON: Of course, sure. Something as delectable as Silver Tinkle just invites stealing. I'll send more, from Riga, but for transport we'll need help from your intelligence people, like before.

MAXIM: Not a problem. Just like before. (unintelligible exchange) His Excellency says it must be this exact product. Obligatory. Not some of your other vodkas. (unintelligible) And hurry, he says.

JACKSON: Of course! We'll expedite it. Maybe we could send some of our superior wine products for his Excellency to try. We have some wonderful items, like—

MAXIM: Wait, wait. Hold please. (unintelligible exchange) No, do not send any wine products. His Excellency feels these are for homosexuals and dissipated peoples.

JACKSON: Okay, fine, that's fine. I'll have a Spodie catalog sent with the Silver Tinkle, in case he would like to peruse it at his leisure and perhaps place an order at a later date.

MAXIM: If you must.

JACKSON: Maxim, please. Be a little more flexible. Ms. Scrotova will not respond well to this kind of closed-mindedness from you, you know.

MAXIM: Of course. No problems. We will talk again. Later. For now, goodbye. (call terminated)

Brewster sipped his wine and shook his head in amazement. "This really is nuts. So we don't know why Yeltsin is so fixated on Silver Tinkle? And what's the story on Nadia being a threat to those guys?"

"I told ya, we don't have the full story yet. But ya gotta admit, this is pretty kick-ass work, hah? Come on, admit it!"

He smiled and clinked glasses with her. "Heidi, you are the best, no question."

She took another swallow of wine, beaming. "Just remember that, when you get your checkbook out, 'kay?" She slid her glass onto the desktop and began rifling through the transcript again. "So I got nothin' between the borscht twins and Boy-tits, and I'm kinda pissed about that. But maybe she only communicates with those guys when she's in Russia? I dunno. I'd love to get some taps goin' over there, but that's outta my league." She slapped a page she just uncovered. "Here ya go, here's another bitchin' little slice of tap heaven. This is your brother and Boy-tits, only ten minutes after that last call you were readin'. Ten minutes!"

JACKSON: Can you talk?

NADIA: Yes. Is good.

JACKSON: It's all taking hold. He wants more.

NADIA: Is great. Soon, he wants it?

JACKSON: He wants forty, as soon as we can get a truck out of Riga.

NADIA: Fantastic. The rest of it is on time. Clockwork.

JACKSON: Perfect. I'm a little worried about Maxim, though. He talks like he doesn't know who he's working for.

NADIA: He thinks he works for other Univod directors. Let me take care of it. Power is in our reach now. If he is so foolish, I have his sack cut off.

The Bat leaned back in her chair, holding her wine. Brewster noted with irritation that she had her pudgy hand on the bowl of the wineglass, not on the stem. She knew better than that. He was sure she was doing it just to aggravate him.

"So I'll keep sluggin' away, but all I got for weapons are the ones I'm usin' now. Surveillance, taps, eavesdroppin'. Like I said, best would be to get bodies workin' on the ground in Russia, but I'm not the fuckin' MI6."

Brewster was thoughtful. "Don't worry about that, you just find out what you can about the vodka, and the relationship between Jock and Nadia and Yeltsin. I'll see what else I can do."

"Check. What I can tell ya is, Butschling is bonin' Boytits all right. You can listen to the tapes if ya like. Pretty boring, though. She gives it the scout try, with her little Russian noises and whatnot, but he's one of those twenty-second guys. Already after about five seconds he's making squeaking noises like—"

"Fine, fine, but what are they up to?"

"It's kinda complicated," she said, slurping some wine. "But the headline is that she wants a favor from him. Somethin' to do with Missus Zorro. I got nothin' specific because they kept talking around it, whatever it is, like they already had the conversation. Musta been before I got my listenin' guys on the job."

The Bat showed Brewster the key parts of the transcript that went along with the tapes.

NADIA: *Pupchin*, we must talk more about my meeting. Pliz say you will do it.

FABRICE: I would do anysing for you, you know zat, but I am worry about zees.

NADIA: Please, please do this one thing. It will be huge relief for me. Good for her, good for you, too.

FABRICE: I am worry zat it will make everysing worse.

NADIA: But is big benefit for all, can you not see?

FABRICE: I will do my best, *chérie*. I would move a mountain for you. Now come to me. Make me happy.

(Rustling of fabric, muffled sounds.)

NADIA: But you must make it work, *pupchin*. I am such ambitious girl, it will mean the world to me. If you move that mountain, it move me, too. Mmmmmm... (inaudible)

DESPERATION CALLING

When the Bat was gone, Brewster picked up the phone. He knew it was a huge risk, but he dialed Dion's direct line at the Control Hub. Dion picked up and gave his coded greeting: "Jeremiah was a bullfrog."

Brewster used his voice distortion device to sound like a gravelly female alto. Protocol demanded that he use the proper code line to identify himself, but instead he said, "I get pushed out of shape and it's hard to steer, when I get rubber in all four gears." It was a code line used only for extraordinary emergencies.

"If you're ever in Alaska, stop in and see my cute little eskimo." Huge relief. Dion knew it was Brewster and was signaling his willingness to talk. So, using lyrics from songs by Dusty Springfield, The Temptations, The Buckinghams, and Mitch Ryder and the Detroit Wheels—among others—Brewster revealed as much as he knew about his brother's involvement in the production of the unusual new vodka that seemed to be affecting the stability of the new Russian Federation at the highest levels.

"If you like Pina Coladas, and getting caught in the rain." Dion wanted more specific, actionable information.

"When I get to Surf City I'll be shootin' the curl, and checkin' out the parties for a surfer girl." Brewster was saying he had nothing more, and that the League should get an operative assigned to the situation to provide some further intel. Dion Agreed.

There was an awkward pause. Both were uneasy about a conversation that was, after all, not sanctioned by the League. Dion said, "I see a red door and I want it painted black." He was saying he would immediately initiate an operation to dose Jock with MLII.

"Bend over, let me see you shake a tail feather," Brewster replied. A strong objection. Then he surprised even himself by adding, "I shot the sheriff, but I did not shoot the deputy." He was saying he would do the job himself.

Another pause, as both absorbed the audacity of the suggestion. Dion pointed out, by way of Bobby Darin, that this was a grave step. Such an action, unless taken in a large gathering like the ones the League preferred, might compromise Brewster's identity as a member. Was he prepared for that? It could mean never resuming his work in the fight for justice in wine and spirits.

"Does your chewing gum lose its flavor on the bedpost overnight?" Brewster was answering in the affirmative. And by adding the line, "How deep is your love, baby?" he asked if Dion, in turn, was prepared to risk exposing the whole organization to international law enforcement.

"Midnight at the oasis, send your camel to bed," he said. And it was done. They had both committed to the venture, whatever it would bring.

Brewster ended the call before Dion could ask him how he had secured ordnance for the proposed operation. He was shaky, his breath shallow. Was he truly going to dose his own brother? Would Dion inform others of the plan? Hideo? The general League membership? As he poured himself more wine, the glass looked strangely small.

CAROLYN SEES ALL

League members did call her Bride of Jockenstein, yes, but the truth was we never knew much about Carolyn. We saw only her odd combination of business-attire counterculturist and motivational cheerleader, with some young Shirley Temple thrown in. It was only during the explosive events of the summer of 1991 that we got more than a superficial look at her.

It was true that she was always happy to be helpful at Spodie International. Her work life at B of A was so defined by corporate structures, stiffly-worded memos, and ice-cold meeting agendas, that she was relieved to have opportunities to help the family, doing something on a human scale. Though it usually involved astrological tips that were received graciously if a little condescendingly, she didn't mind. Bringing computers to Spodie International was another of those moments that made her feel good, and because it was something so related to the nuts-and-bolts side of business, she knew the family thought more of it than of her astrological contributions. It was satisfying for her initially, at least—until Jock began spending more and more time in front of his computer at home and his travels to Moscow became so much more frequent. She was amazed (and a little dismayed) when he got one of the new

portable computers—this was when laptops were a futur-
istic wonder—and took it with him on his travels. Soon
she was seeing stacks of floppy disks on his desk at home,
many marked only with the words "the project" followed
by a roman numeral. At first it was something Carolyn noticed only in the softest sense, like she would notice the
color of his tie.

When first she asked him about it, he gave her a blank
look, followed by an indulgent smile. Of course it was
nothing out of the ordinary. He would tell her if it was,
wouldn't he? Shortly after, the disks disappeared from his
desk. Was he just tidying up, she wondered? Out of idle
curiosity (she told herself), one day she checked his desk
drawers. Office supplies, company stationery, blank disks,
lunch-size bag of Cheezows. Had the middle drawer, with
the lock, always been locked? She wasn't sure. When she
asked again about the "project," he reassured her that it
was just a long term study of labels and graphics, meant to
give Spodie's brands an advantage in the marketplace. It
was focus group and phone survey data, no big deal. And
the trips to Russia were aimed at getting a foot in the door
of Eastern European markets when they finally opened
up—which would be soon! Exciting!

"Does Nadia whats-her-name go along with you?"
Carolyn said, during one discussion.

Jock laughed. "No way! She's a tough cookie, that one.
I steer clear of her, let me tell you. I'm always afraid she'll
hurt me if I don't like her ideas!"

"But it could be dangerous over in Russia now, sweetie," she said. "What with Germany up in the air, and all
those Soviet republics screaming for independence, it just

seems so unstable. You know?" She was almost pleading with him. "And I've been looking at progressions on the Soviet Union's natal chart. It looks scary, Jock. The dispositor of the chart is Saturn, and we are looking at a square with Neptune that will last for years; and Mars square to Jupiter in Virgo on top of that. Lots of volatility and delusion, maybe violence."

Jock dismissed her fears, but they stayed with her, along with niggling questions, hanging in the air.

It was on the 27th of August that Carolyn's curiosity got the better of her. Our information confirmed that she'd taken the afternoon off and had just had lunch, including drinks and a bottle of wine, with a friend from the Junior League, so she was feeling no pain when she got home. She walked past the open door of Jock's office. She hesitated, then lurched in toward the desk. She booted up the computer. Desk drawer still locked. Shocking herself, she picked up the letter opener on the desk top and tried to force the drawer. It groaned, but held fast. She scurried into the kitchen, as if trying to stay ahead of her thoughts. From a bottom drawer that held tools, she took a screw driver and a hammer. She was unsteady enough that the first strike of the hammer glanced off the screw driver and dented the desk's finish, but three more blows splintered the drawer's top edge and the lock gave way. The disks were there, more than a dozen. She was in a cold sweat as she fed one into the computer and was confronted with notes describing the vodka project, translated by Nadia. She looked at the contents of another disk, then another, piecing together the story of Silver Tinkle. She was astonished, but it was the fourth disk that set her hands to shaking. It was a blueprint of Nadia and Jock's plan to pull an end-run on Univod itself and hijack the fledgling Russian government, as the Soviet Union disintegrated. On the same disk was a summary schedule of Jock's trips to Moscow and Riga since the previous December—accompanied on all of them by Nadia.

Her breathing was fast and shallow. She didn't bother turning off the computer, but picked up the desk phone, then slammed it down. Barely able to lock the front door, she sped down to the Spodie offices on lower Fillmore. She cursed as she drove up to the entrance—there was never any parking—and ended up leaving her car in a loading zone. She shot right past Candace, the receptionist, whose welcoming smile turned to horror when she realized Carolyn was going straight into Jock's office.

We have only the murkiest picture of what she found there, because of starkly conflicting, not to mention self-serving, narratives. What is certain: Jock was reclining on the office sectional, his belt unfastened, pants unzipped. He later said he had consumed huge quantities of Cheezows and was just relaxing and "relieving some pressure" as he wrapped up his meeting with Nadia. Nadia herself was on her knees between the coffee table and sofa, close to Jock. She later insisted that she had spilled her drink and was in the process of mopping up. Whatever the case, the tableau was enough to send Carolyn into a blood rage. The dialogue is primarily from her recollections.

"I can't believe this! You evil bastard! Now I get the truth! You, with your Mercury conjunct Venus in Scorpio squared to your moon…and to Jupiter! I should have known! I wanted your other placements to compensate, I wanted to believe they could." Her chin trembled as if she might sob, but when her eyes locked on Nadia she snapped back to pure fury. "And with this slut! This bitch, this whore! That's right, I said *whore*—don't look so shocked!"

Jock's eyes showed pure fear, but he tried on a weak smile. "Now wait, sweetheart, you're making this—"

She picked up a crystal vase full of yellow roses that had been on a side table, and tossed it at him, hitting his right shoulder, then the carpeted floor without breaking.

"Oh Jesus, don't make it worse for yourself. You are such a *shit*! I can't believe I trusted you, all this time! Your wife, me, I mean nothing to you!" She felt a sob rising in her throat, and bolted for the door. She drove off just as Jock got out to the curb, shirttails flapping, fly unzipped.

Back in the office, he assessed the damage with Nadia. The only real question was whether her visit had been coincidental. Had she looked at his computer files?

"It was bad luck for you, nothing more," said Nadia. "I think she knows nothing."

"You might be right. But you might not. All the more reason for us to plow ahead with the program, full speed. With the kidnapping, too." He looked puzzled. "She never goes through my stuff, ever! I guess she could have looked at my computer—but why wouldn't she have done it before?"

"You didn't put a password lock on your computer?" said Nadia.

He looked blank. "You can do that?"

"Focking hell," she said.

He went to his desk and called home to leave a message, pleading with her to at least hear him out. He loved her so much. This was a misunderstanding.

CAROLYN UNCHAINED

We know that on the morning of the 27th, Brewster tasted wine with Margot as usual.

"I've got to be outta here right after we finish, though," she told him. "I've got that tastin' at one o'clock."

"I know, I know. The Bay Club." He was distracted and grumpy as they sat down in front of two rows of glasses.

"Well you don't have to talk about it like it's a damn adult circumcision. You said I should do it. Not to mention it's two-thousand bucks in the bank."

"Yes, right. All true. It's just that those old jackals in their Brooks Brothers sportswear don't know which end of the bottle to open. But they're just like anyone else—waiting for you to perform your miracles so they can say they saw it all, and then get drunk on the leftovers."

"What about tomorrow? Here I thought you'd be all excited about it. I'm nervous as hell."

"Margot, I *am* excited; why are you bitching at me? The tasting kit is going to take off after this interview. Are you kidding? Do you know how many viewers they pull in on Morning Noise? About a hundred thousand. It's going to bring people to your door, I can tell you. A whole flock of new endorsements. You can be selling frozen lasagna before the month is over if you want." He picked up a glass and sniffed. "God but I hate Cab Franc. It might be a good blender, but as a leading player it sucks."

"Brewster, you are wound up tighter than a tick! Why don't you just relax and do some tasting? We're wasting time here."

"Have you seen Heidi's people hanging around? Are they taking care of you?"

Margot scowled. "How the hell am I supposed to know? She said herself I wouldn't notice anybody followin' me. I guess they're out there somewhere, I dunno. You're drivin' me up a wall! Here you are complainin' and worryin' about every little thing, and if times got any better for me I'd have to hire somebody to help me enjoy 'em."

After a quick lunch sitting at the Coup de Food bar, he went back to the office, feeling too glum to do much of anything. Sipping a glass of Sauternes, he tried to rough out a two thousand-word piece he owed to the wine magazine *Guzzler,* about the newest, most expensive crystal wine glasses available, made in a special secret laboratory/factory located in high orbit around the earth. The company was called Space Grail, Inc., and its owners—a Swiss physicist, an Israeli chemist, and an Indian guru named Babu Verananda—insisted that the $1000 per glass retail price was low, considering unit costs and the ultimate result. Only in zero gravity, they said, could crystal stemware of such perfect weight, shape, and optical perfection be produced. They couldn't keep up with demand.

Every sentence he wrote looked like gibberish. He napped for an hour sitting in his chair, waking finally to the phone ringing. He clutched his stiff neck with one hand and grabbed the phone with the other.

It was Carolyn.

"Brewster? Listen to me." Her voice shook. "I've just discovered some things that are very shocking, but I don't want to go to Mum about any of it, so I'm calling you."

"What do you mean? Where's Jock?"

"Somewhere he shouldn't be. The son of a bitch. But I'm not...I'm not discussing that. What I found out is that Silver Tinkle is being supplied right now, in quantity, to the head of the Russian government. You saw the news a couple of days ago about Boris Yeltsin, standing up on a tank and facing down some kind of coup attempt?"

"Sure I did, it was hard to miss."

"Well, it looks like he was sloshed on Silver Tinkle while he did it. In fact, he's probably on a steady diet of the stuff. I'd try the same regimen for myself...if...if I thought it would do any good!" She began to sob.

"Carolyn, slow down here. What happened? You sound terrible."

She finally got the story out. She used language he had never heard from her before, including one of his least favorite words for female genitalia. He expected to hear the news the Bat had already told him, but it turned out that she had much more. She had discovered the secret of Silver Tinkle: why it was so different from competitors, why Yeltsin was already such a loyal fan, and the part it played in Jock and Nadia's ultimate game plan.

"They're—they're planning to control Russia. Dictators basically," she said, gulping for air. "Now that the Soviet Union in gone, they're consolidating their coup—an alcoholic coup! I should probably be calling the CIA or something! It's just—"

"Hold on, hold on a second. You're not making sense. What does Silver Tinkle have to do with all this?"

"Okay, yes. I'm not focusing too well. My transiting Mercury is retrograde in Pisces, and it's just—just pretty shitty. There are reams of stuff about this in Jock's computer files, but the bottom line is that the vodka is made from special wheat."

"But so what? I mean, who cares? Special wheat is in Special K, too."

"No, no, this wheat's been genetically modified. You know what that is? Okay, because I didn't. The stuff has been hybridized in Latvia, by some guys Jock met four or five years ago at Univod in Moscow. That bastard has been at this for years behind everyone's back—except that scum slut, of course! But here's the strange part: the genetic materials they put in the wheat are from the coca leaf and from silk worms. So they've got something that acts as a powerful depressant and a stimulant at the same time! And the silkworm material supposedly makes the stuff unbelievably smooth."

Brewster was dumbfounded. He talked a little longer with Carolyn, getting details about the timeline. And he let her vent. He reassured her that he would handle the situation with Jock, minimizing the problems with Mum and damage to the company in the media.

"That's great. I know your natal Mars in Gemini, trine to Jupiter in Aquarius, will get this done. I don't want Mum to be blindsided and shocked by everything.

But I don't give a shit what happens to him! He—he sold me out! That evil shit!" Her breathing sounded like a steam engine. "I'm going to a hotel. I'll be in touch. I've got the floppy discs, and I'm taking them with me."

"What hotel, in case I need to get in touch?"

"Never mind. I'm going to feel safer if no one knows where I am. I'll call you."

He barely had time to give her his cell number before she hung up.

He called the Bat and told her the story, insisting that she focus now only on whatever Nadia and Fabrice were cooking up.

"Whatever you say, Brew. You're writin' the checks. Shit, so your brother's a huge dickwad. Who'd ever guess, hah?" A moment of awkward silence. "But I'm still keeping an eye on Cleopatra, right? I just got word that she's on her way back from the Pacific Club."

"Right, great. Call me when there's news."

He wanted to call Margot and tell her the whole story. But why? He realized it would serve no purpose, other than to fray her nerves and blow her anti-vodka rage through the roof. And he knew the call would actually be intended to pump up his image in her eyes, reduce his terrible feeling of his own bon vivant superfluity in the world. The way Bernadette had always looked at him.

Jock rushed home, arriving sometime after 4 p.m. He groaned and slammed the wall with his fist when he rounded the corner and saw his desk drawer hanging open, tools on the floor. Did Carolyn know everything, then? Did she bother looking at the project details? Did she see his travel schedule with Nadia? Where was she? He dialed Nadia's number from his desk phone. "Bad news," he said, when she picked up. "Carolyn has the disks."

"Shit!" she spat out, in spite of herself. Taking a deep breath, she said, "Don't let us talk now. Let's meet later, at Union Square. Nine o'clock." Nadia was shaken, of course, fearful that in her rage Carolyn might have gone to someone who could make trouble for them. Mum? So What? Law enforcement? No one there would take her seriously—what was the crime? But still: better to play it safe. Minimal phone conversation, discussions carried on outdoors or in safe locations.

A BAD MOOD, ENCODED

Brewster called Dion's direct line again and laid out the situation, this time using lyrics from Glenn Campbell, the Partridge Family, the Village People, Sam the Sham and the Pharaohs, and Bobby Vee.

Dion was clearly stupified to hear about the modified wheat, the vodka production and storage in Latvia. "I write the songs that make the young girls cry," he said, indicating a desire for a face-to-face meeting.

"There's a kind of hush all over the world," said Brewster, using a Herman's Hermits classic to state that he had his hands full and could not agree to Dion's request.

Dion was adamant. "Come on and turn it on, wind it up, blow it out GTO," he said.

Brewster let Dion know that the League's best move was to try to find whatever stocks of Silver Tinkle were left in Riga and destroy them. He told him further, via David Bowie and Abba, that he still intended to dose his brother. Dion asked for assurances that the operation would maintain everyone's anonymity.

Brewster replied, "You're gonna need an ocean of calamine lotion." Which was to say he would provide no such assurance. He felt the operation was urgent and needed to be carried out soon, however it could be accomplished.

The last of their exchange was quite angry—though of course the encoding precluded much emotional shading. Brewster knew Dion was exercised when he signed off with "You probably think this song is about you," an unambiguous code line for "dissatisfaction/no agreement."

Unlocking the bottom desk drawer, he pulled out the plastic bottle that held the mix of Zipp and MLII and set it on the desk like a talisman. He wanted to call Jock, but what could he say that wouldn't send up an alarm? He wanted to call Margot. He called Margot.

"So. Did it go well, the Pacific Club?"

"Yeah, it was all right. Too many pink oxford shirts for me, though. And the breath on some of those guys. Drop a white rhino at twenty paces. So did you call just to ask about that? I'm doubtin' it."

"Good guess. So how about getting some dinner in an hour or so? At the Coup de Food?"

"Thanks for the thought and all, but I'm weedin' a pretty wide row here. I've got to go over the notes for the interview tomorrow—the ones you gave me, remember?—plus I'm trying to put together my tasting program for next week."

"So you're not going out?"

She was exasperated. "No, Brewster, I'm not. You wanna put some kinda tracking contraption on me? A chastity belt? What? You already have Heidi campin' on my porch, practically. *Sacré casse-pieds, toi*!"

"Now take it easy, Margot. I'm just concerned about your safety, that's all."

"Right, well my safety right now looks like finishin' my work here and getting a good night's sleep."

So Brewster went to dinner alone, as he so often did. Feeling frazzled and sorry for himself, he made certain to drink enough wine to soften the impact of a fateful day, and the prospect of more on the horizon.

FABRICE THE TOOL

The fact was that when Brewster called her, Margot had just gotten off the phone with Fabrice. She had agreed to have dinner with him the following night at the Gravy Stain.

"Ooh, I been interested in tryin' that place," she said.

"I am as well. Eet eez a very good reputation. And I 'ave more business to discuss wiss you, somesing you will like."

"I guess we're gonna have to talk about your 'Alsassy' project, too, Fabrice. Those jerks at Spodie aren't gonna do you any big favors. They're crooked as a barrel full of snakes. I want to talk to you about maybe doin' less."

"Please, take no decision now. We will talk tomorrow. You must be comfortable, *chérie*, I would not want eet to be ozerwise. You can meet me at nine?" He of course said nothing about Nadia. He didn't even mention the "major industry figure" who wanted to meet with Margot. Why cause unnecessary trouble? The goal was that she should hear the business opportunities once she is there and comfortable with Nadia. She would thank him later.

Margot told herself she would not tell Brewster about the dinner; it would just launch him into another conniption of passive-aggressive jealousy.

Fabrice was jubilant when he called Nadia's office at Multishots, around 4 p.m. He started to tell her that the dinner with Margot was set, but she cut him off.

"Please, *pupchin*, let us talk when we get together for dinner—you will come here? In two hours, is okay with you?"

When Fabrice arrived at Multishots, he was surprised to find Nadia waiting for him in the lobby. She took him by the arm and led him out the door, smiling lazily all the while.

"Look at you! You look so delicious today, *chérie*. I could eat *you* for dinnair!" He laughed. "But maybe we go to a resto instead, what do you say?"

She steered them to Jaw Music, a big, noisy bistro three blocks away, where zydeco caromed off hard surfaces and successfully competed with patrons' raised voices. Even sophisticated eavesdropping equipment would be useless. As they eased between the crowded tables, Fabrice looked unhappy. He thought they would have to get through the meal shouting at each other, but once seated Nadia leaned across the small table and put her lips near his ear. "For me, this is sexiest thing. In big crowd, but so intimate." She flicked her tongue in his ear.

He smiled knowingly, hunching over the table to reach her ear. "You are so *exquise*, Nadia *chérie*. How will I keep my hands off you long enough to eat my *moules-frites*?" They both laughed. "But I have such good news! Margot eez coming to dinnair tomorrow evening!"

Nadia's eyes lit up as they seldom did. As best she could, she took both of his huge hands in hers. "Oh, *pupchin*, that is wonderful! You melt my heart! I quiver inside just to touch you!" A sigh. "You will pick me up at the office, maybe 8:45?"

"At your command, of course."

"But now—we celebrate!"

"*Absolument*! But tell me: what are some of zeez opportunities you wish to talk to 'er about?"

She smiled broadly. "That, *pupchin*, will be a surprise."

As they finished dinner, Fabrice clutched her knee under the table. "Ah, *ma petite noisette entière*, I am now longing to enjoy my dessert! You will come back to zee hotel weez me, of course?"

She begged off, saying she had a mountain of work to do. Back at the office, she made one call, lasting only a few seconds. When she heard the receiver being lifted, she said only "What a nice day" before hanging up.

It was a mild summer night, and crowds of people milled around Union Square, tourists with shopping bags, musicians, loiterers.

"So are we on?" Jock said, breathless as he approached her.

"Come with me." She barely made eye contact with him. She led him across the street to Macy's, where they stood among racks of women's sportswear and spoke in low tones.

"Do you really think all this is necessary?" he said. "The CIA doesn't know we exist."

"That is what you say." She looked at him coldly. "You are so worried because your wife might leave you. I worry because our plan for the wodka, for Russia itself, is at stake. Don't tell me to not worry." She glared at him for a moment. "So she has the disks? Where is she?"

"Yes. I don't know where she is," he said, trying to manage his panic.

"You are real idiot, you know. But I think is best to go ahead with plan for Sipski."

"We're on, then?"

"Yes, tomorrow at 9 p.m."

"That's a relief."

"So happy to provide relief for idiots. From what I saw of your wife, she is too weak to make much trouble. What she can do, call your mother?"

"She can't even do that. Mum is down in Carmel visiting friends."

"Good." She feigned interest in some blouses on the rack.

"Those are disgusting," he said.

"Don't worry. Nothing in your size." She confirmed the details of the kidnapping. Three Moroccans. Margot would be taken to the newest of the South City warehouses, which as yet contained no inventory and was awaiting permits. A ransom demand would be phoned in anonymously to KGO and KPIX.

"You'll be there?" he asked.

"Yes. And you will not."

He nodded. "I'm going to get Brewster out of the way."

"You will kill him?"

"Jesus, Nadia, you are one bloodthirsty bitch."

"I did not get to this place by being Mother Teresa. You will drug him, or what?"

"Something like that. I've got the perfect bait. Some old Bordeaux wines I found through a buddy of mine. Brewster's such a wine boozer, he won't be able to resist coming over to try 'em. And I'm taking the precaution of slipping some Quaaludes into the glasses, to make sure he goes out. This is air tight. Just be sure your guys get that cell phone away from Sipski first thing. She could try a 911 call. She'll never get a hold of Brewster by then, that's for sure."

BORDEAUX BAIT

Based on phone records, it was about 10:30 when Jock got home. His heart sank when he saw the house was dark. He went up to the bedroom hoping crazily that Carolyn might be there asleep, but there was just a neatly-made bed. He listened to messages on the answering machine, three of them his own, pleading with her to call him when she got home. He went into his study, poured himself a generous tumbler of expensive bourbon (distributed by a competitor), and dropped into an overstuffed chair. He dialed his brother's number, but because Brewster was lingering at the bar at the Coup de Food, the call went to his answering machine.

Taking a deep breath and trying to sound casual, he said, "Hey Nipper, this is your big brother. Listen, I've got some great news for you—well, for Mum, actually. Through a buddy of mine, Rich Jollyfinger—remember him? From the First Presbyterian toga party a couple of years ago?—-anyway, he told me about some amazing old Bordeaux he was selling and I thought maybe I'd buy a few bottles of this and that for Mum's cellar. And that's where you come in. I wanna see if I can get you over here tomorrow night to taste 'em, and tell me what you think. We'd have you come for dinner, but Carolyn is working late and I'm completely buried. I'm thinking eight o'clock or so. Let me know."

When Brewster got home and heard the message, he called Jock though it was after 11. He'd had plenty of wine plus a couple of snifters of Louis XIX cognac, so he wasn't feeling much in the way of inhibitions. He was nervous, yes: shocked by Carolyn's account of Jock's actions, fearful of what he might do next. Also torn between seeing this as a golden opportunity to dose his brother, and the possibility that the encounter would out him as a League operative.

"So. These wines you found. What are we talking about?"

"Okay, so there's two vintages from three different chateaux, and Rich says he has four or five bottles of each. I gave him a thousand bucks each for one bottle of all six, plus first refusal on the rest at eight hundred a bottle. I don't know how good this shit is—hell, nobody knows, they're so damn old—but I figured Mum might get a thrill out of 'em. They're from, ah, 1870 and 1874. He said they're 'pre-phylloxera.' So that must be Latin for 'really old'? Rich told me they even had new corks put in 'em about forty years ago."

Brewster's mind was surging and sputtering, racing on cognac fumes, but he held himself in check. As coherently as he could, he explained that all those wines, if they were authentic, were made before the phylloxera root louse devastated Europe's vineyards at the end of the 19th century, forcing growers to replant all their vineyards using American rootstocks that were resistant to the louse. "Those old vines produced some of the greatest wines ever," he said. What chateaux? Come on. Gimme some details."

"Okay, relax. The labels are all in shitty condition. Jollyfinger said the wine was in some old London cellar since forever. But most of 'em are from big names—Chateau Fargaux and Chateau Pontificat. Everybody's heard of them. There's also some from Vieux Chateau Pétanque, wherever that is."

More excited than ever—they really were great names—Brewster said he would be there the following night. "You should have Mum in on this. She'll be excited."

"Mum's out of town. Which you would know if you called her more often. She's down in Carmel for a couple of nights visiting the Reardons."

"Great. Yes, and thanks for channeling a little shot of guilt from her. Almost a good as the real thing. Maybe you should try bottling some of that for test marketing, huh?"

"Bye, Nipper."

At six the next morning, a hung-over Brewster drove Margot to the KFIC studios on Mission Street for the Morning Noise interview. He wanted to tell her about the old Bordeaux Jock had, but he knew it would just unleash her temper, getting her back onto the topics of Jock and Isopropov. Anyway, she was already as frazzled as he had ever seen her, asking him in the space of a minute to turn the heat on, then off. She hummed "Ring of Fire" for most of the ride, stopping only when Brewster spoke to her.

"You know the best way to relieve tension like this, don't you?" he asked.

"Sure I do. But I generally don't stroke my own banjo."

"Oh come on, Margot, why are you being so difficult?

We've been friends for years now! Am I that repulsive to you?"

"Are we there yet?"

She got a full seven minutes of airtime, generous for the show's normal format. She parried a few questions about her background, talked a bit about her triumph in the French television tasting show, and then, to Brewster's relief, got right into the topic of the tasting kit. The specially designed glasses, the wine evaluation sheet she'd designed, the corkscrew engraved with her signature. The host turned out to be supportive and jovial ("I can't tell Cabernet from carbonated"), which helped put her at ease as she described the truly unique part of the kit: tongue dye sheets. Tasters were instructed to put the sheet on their tongues for a few moments, then compare the transferred image of taste buds—both location and number—to the laminated similar image of Margot's taste buds. Find out how your buds stack up to the Master's!

Finally, with Brewster cringing as she spoke, there was the No-Vodka Pledge. He had tried to talk her out of including it in the kit, but had gotten nowhere.

"Vodka makes about as much sense as a trap door in a canoe, and I'm not shy about sayin' it. I'm askin' anybody who wants to join my little club to sign a pledge to give it up, whether it's bein' served straight or in some crazy mess of a mixed drink." The show's host asked her if that didn't seem a little extreme, what with all the vodka drinkers in the world; and it was then, in the last ninety seconds of the interview, that Margot got heated.

"Let me tell you somethin': I am never gonna be casual about somethin' as stupid and meaningless as vodka.

It's a sensory deprivation project from the get-go; kinda like fragrance-free perfume, if anyone was dumb enough to make it, and if perfume could get you shit-faced. If you're just interested in deadenin' your senses, then be my guest; most vodka lovers can't find their butts with two hands and a search warrant, anyway. I just don't want anybody to join my club if they don't care about flavor. And it doesn't matter whether you're talkin' about the pricey vodkas or the rot-gut…"

Once they were outside, Margot admitted she might have gotten a little harsh.

"A little!" Brewster grabbed her shoulder and shook it. "You do remember somebody took a shot at you not long ago, right? And vodka people are at the top of the suspect list."

"They just shot a damn window, Brewster. And the cops never came up with any suspects, I told you." She pulled away and elbowed him, smiling a little. "Maybe your brother did it, how about that?"

"Don't even joke. How about having some dinner with me tonight?"

"Sorry," she grinned. "I'm in demand."

"I'll bet it's Butschling."

She gave him a mocking smile. "Don't even joke."

HOTTE BROTHERS

The Gravy Stain exploded onto the San Francisco food scene in 1991, fueled by some excellent reviews and raves from a few sports and movie figures in the Bay Area. Built out from an old diner, the building was low-slung and homey, with clapboard siding and shutters. It was almost directly beneath a freeway overpass which for much of the day kept whatever sun there was from reaching it. On one side was O'Toole's Tools, a defunct equipment rental company, and on the other a tire sales and repair operation, featuring piles of huge truck tires, old and cracked, stacked against the stucco wall of the shop like gigantic malodorous bagels.

The restaurant was a paradise of fashionable reverse snobbery. The owner, an aging hippy philosophy major at Cornell, had discovered Europe and its cuisines as he toured around on his bicycle. His wife, whom he met on his tour, was French. There were two large dining rooms, both with mismatched tables swathed in oilcloth, and folding chairs. Window views were of chain link fences and industrial flotsam. Simple dishes such as *petit salé* were advertised on the menu as being made with house-made sausages and smoked ham, Le Puy lentils, sweet onion from Hawaii and vegetables grown by cloistered nuns in a monastery garden outside of San Clamato, a half hour north of San Francisco.

But as Jock and Nadia agreed, the choice of the Gravy Stain involved more than its trendy image and food, items likely to attract Margot. It also involved a parking lot with strategic advantages. It was large, about half of it paved, the other half crushed shale that had previously belonged to the equipment rental operation. All of it was poorly lit, and if Fabrice parked far out enough, if the kidnappers were positioned just so, it would be a simple matter to get some duct tape first on Margot' mouth, then on her wrists and ankles, and speed her to a safe house.

At exactly 8 p.m. that night, Brewster rang the bell at Mum's house and let himself in. Jock emerged from the study, drink in hand.

"Hey, Nipper. Glad you made it." His smile was wan. "I won't offer you a bourbon since you're gonna want to focus on the wines, right? I know you." He slapped Brewster awkwardly on the shoulder.

"Fine by me. You're doing well?" Brewster sounded nervous even to his own ears. As if he hadn't reflected on it before, he realized the obvious: now that he was there, with Jock, just the two of them, it would be impossible for him to abort the operation. It was too close, too tantalizing. Even with the chance that the League itself might be compromised. He was, after all, standing a few feet from his brother, a person shaping up to be among the most notorious characters ever to earn full Prick status with the League.

"I'm doin' great, great. Things are pretty busy,

thankfully. All those new launches keepin' us hopping. We're makin' money for ya!" He gestured for Brewster to proceed him out of the entry hall to a door under the grand staircase. Brewster opened it and they made their way down to the basement. He involuntarily fingered his signet ring, where he had put the dose intended for Jock.

Mum's cellar was an ornate wine mausoleum, the cold room and its racks done in redwood with cherry accents, the floor in white Carrara marble. The tasting area itself held a dark 16th century French refectory table for sit-down affairs, as well as a raised round table, close by the cold room, for less formal tasting. It was here that Jock had set out six bottles, with two sets of six glasses. There was a decanter for each bottle, along with an assortment of corkscrews.

"I think it's best not to decant these guys, unless the corks don't hold together," said Brewster. He looked at the bottles. "They're beauties. They've been down here for a week?"

"Yeah. And like I said, according to Jollyfinger they've had really good storage." He gestured toward the table. "Figured I'd leave the job of opening 'em to you," said Jock. "You're the pro. You handle 'em any way you like."

Brewster smiled grimly. "You want me to take the blame for a bunch of crumbling corks, is that it?"

Jock laughed nervously. "Something like that, yeah."

Brewster uncorked the wines, four relatively easily, while two corks disintegrated and forced him to use cheese-cloth to strain the wine into decanters. He suggested they taste those two first. Chateau Fargaux 1870 and Pontificat 1874.

"Pretty good color on both of these," said Brewster, excited in spite of himself. "I'm a little nervous just pouring them."

Jock's eyes were everywhere but on the wines. "Uh, yeah, absolutely. Nice color. I mean, for their age and all."

They tasted, and Brewster let out a little yelp. "The 1870 is amazing! A little leathery, but still some nice, floral potpourri fruit. And it still has some length!" He looked up at Jock. "Mind if I pour myself some more?"

"No, no, go right ahead," said Jock heartily. "That's what it's here for. I mean, why not?"

With the exception of the Vieux Chateau Pétanque '74, all the wines were holding up well, Brewster announced; as they chatted he went back to refresh his glass several times on all of them.

"Go ahead," said Jock. "It's a shame to let 'em go to waste."

FULL BLADDER TAILING

The Bat took over surveillance of Margot's place around 5 p.m., one hour earlier than scheduled. She'd just come from teaching her master class at the Taekwondo Academy on Geary, so she was still in her togs and not very happy that she'd only had time to get a take-out meatball sandwich from Friggini's, the café next to the academy where she often had dinner after class.

"What d'ya got?" she asked, when she got to the spot where her friend Minnie was parked, on Faust Street, a half block from 24th Street and across from Margot's place. Minnie was a forty-ish voice-over performer the Bat had recruited a couple of years before, when she was looking for ways to augment her income. She had called the Bat around noon and told her she needed to leave early. It was an audition. "Gotta keep kissing frogs," she'd told her.

"I've got nothing. Zero," said Minnie. "Subject came in like you said she would, around three. Nothing since then, in or out. I'm pretty sure my colon has fallen out, though. It hit the car floor after I ate one of those GutBusters from Beef-aroo Boys. Like a stone, I swear."

"Hey, great, now you can audition, then go home and pump you stomach or whatever. Gimme your log. You're back on tomorrow six to midnight, right?"

When Minnie was gone, the Bat settled into her routine. She reclined her seat a bit, turned on her little radio, tuned to a light rock station. She grudgingly accepted the meatball sandwich into the routine—after a couple of bites, she even admitted it was pretty good. Just before she left Friggini's with her sandwich, she had heard from her eavesdropping team that Nadia and Fabrice were not together that afternoon. With listening equipment trained on Nadia's office, they picked up the usual calls from vodka distributors around in the country, asking for a visit or promotional support. She made a couple of calls in some patois of Russian, but they were all in the local calling area. They reported one very short call which was odd. She initiated it, the respondent said nothing when they picked up, and she said only "What a nice day" before hanging up.

It was 8:45, the summer light was fading and her bladder was telling her she shouldn't have drunk the whole gigantic ice tea she'd bought to wash down her sandwich. She was just thinking about taking the short walk to the restrooms at the Caffiend when she saw Margot's garage door open and her blue Peugeot nose out of its basement space, drop down the short, narrow driveway onto 24th heading east toward the Mission. Margot was alone in the car.

The Bat sat up and turned on the ignition. She grabbed the cell phone Brewster had given her and punched in his number. She pulled out into traffic. The phone rang twice, and she heard a click. "The person you are trying to reach is either unavailable, or out of the calling area…" She didn't know Brewster was in a cellar, where there was no signal. She punched the button to end the call and dialed his office.

Answering machine. "Where the hell are ya, Brew?" she muttered.

Why hadn't Margot told Brewster—or her—she was going out? She couldn't let her slip away now—even if it meant driving with an exploding bladder.

She followed at a two-car distance, which would have been considered risky if she cared whether Margot saw her. She figured she was going out to dinner, but why so secretive? Margot turned left onto Guerrero. The Bat tried Brewster's cell number again. Same nothing. She followed as Margot turned right onto Thirteenth.

"What the hell you doin' down *here*? Armpit of the whole fuckin' city!" she muttered to herself. "Wherever you're goin', I'm headin' for their crapper first, that's for sure. Or I'm pissin' on a telephone pole."

Nadia had made a few last minute changes to the kidnapping plan. Most significantly, she decided to have two additional men, burly American types, create a drunken commotion just inside the restaurant entrance, at exactly 8:57. It would serve as a diversion and would prevent anyone from leaving during the crucial three to four minutes they needed to get Margot out of the way.

Her people had strict instructions and had been well-rehearsed; she was not very worried. Still, out of an abundance of caution, that afternoon she had called one of her Russian contacts and asked him, in the dialect of her home village near the Ukraine border, to make a shuttle reservation for 11 p.m. that evening, and an Aeroflot reservation for the following morning, Los Angeles to Moscow. She had him use the name on one of her several alternative passports. You never know when you might need an escape hatch.

At 7:15, she decided on a light dinner at Burnum Yankee, a favorite Cajun restaurant near the office. She would be back in plenty of time to meet Fabrice at 8:45. Enjoying her catfish ceviche, she vaguely wondered how Jock was faring with his dunce of a brother.

THE DOSES

Jock made his move when he saw Brewster graduating from delicate sips to more liberal swigging.

"Hey Nipper, I almost forgot. I picked up a couple of cases of Burgundies for Mum last week. Older vintages of—Moosigny, is that it? From a producer by the name of Piquette?"

Brewster put his glass down and turned to Jock. "Seriously? From Olivier Piquette?"

"Yeah! Yeah, that's the one. You want to take a look?"

"Absolutely."

Jock produced the key to the cool room. "I thought you might be interested. Lemme just open things up for you. I put 'em on the right wall, just about in the middle. I think it's bin eleven, twelve, and thirteen."

While Brewster was looking over the Burgundies, exclaiming to himself, Jock had plenty of time to distribute his Quaalude powder in two of Brewster's glasses. The ones he would most certainly drain: the Fargaux 1870 and '74. The white powder dispersed. It nearly disappeared after two short swirls; a few grains of residue clung to the inside of each glass. Brewster would never notice.

Brewster emerged, shaking his head. "Fantastic stuff. Those couple of bottles of '49 must be worth a thousand dollars each. But I gotta tell you, I only found twenty bottles total in those bins. Are you sure you got two full cases?"

Jock grimaced. "Nipper, are you shitfaced already? I was sure you knew how to count. Come on, I put 'em in there myself."

"Well, maybe you can find them. I sure as hell couldn't."

"Jesus, Nipper. I swear." Jock frowned and walked into the cool room, leaving the door ajar.

"Maybe I wasn't looking in the right bins, I dunno," said Brewster loudly. At the same time, he popped open his signet ring and, trembling a little, split the contents between Jock's glasses of Fargaux 1870 and '74. Easily a full dose in each glass. He could feel his cheeks getting numb.

"Nipper, get in here," Jock barked. "The damn wines are right where I said they were."

When they had finished counting bottles and Brewster had shrugged off his mistake, they stood at the table again, sipping and smelling. Both agreed that the Fargaux 1870 was extraordinary.

"Amazing vigor in it," said Brewster. "A hundred and twenty years old, can you believe that? Wonderful spicy notes. Sweet tobacco, anise, toffee. Are you getting any of that?" He raised his glass and sipped, his eyes encouraging Jock to do the same.

Jock picked up his glass, smiled smugly, took a healthy swallow. "You know me, I just like what I like. I describe most pricey wines like Marvin does: shit with a good back-story. But I sure as hell like this shit! This'll knock your dick in the dirt." He emptied his glass. "How about some more?"

"Can't refuse that offer," said Brewster.

"You know, Nipper, I feel like we should be drinking a toast to your friend Margot and her endorsement deal with us."

"Excuse me?"

"You know, with the Butschlings, for the new Alsassy line."

Brewster's stomach went steely cold, but his brain flared into fire. "Don't tell me that. That's bullshit. Margot would never go through with that deal. Never," he said tersely.

"Not according to Fabrice. He says she's on board and ready to start with a photo shoot next week." He smile broadly, then drained his glass.

"That's a lie. And I can prove it right…right now." He glared at Jock, fumbling, trying to fish the bulky cell phone out of his jacket pocket. His fingers were spastic and unco-operative as he punched in Margot's number.

Jock looked amused. He tossed off the Fargaux 1870, and set the glass on the table with a flourish. "I don't think it'll work down here in the cellar, Nipper."

Brewster's eyes were fixed on Jock's lips. That little grin, he hated it. He wanted to punch it, pound it with a meat tenderizer. But he realized it would take more energy than he had right then. In fact, his head seemed to be lolling to the left. Very definitely. To the left. "I think I'm gonna go sit down for a…just a minute." He managed the few steps to the larger table, carrying his glass of Fargaux 1870. He set it down with exaggerated care. "Why? Why do you even want Margot to…do your…stuff? Huh? You hate her. And she's—she's too good…for your shitty program, any-way. Admit it. C'mon!"

"The only thing I'm going to admit, Nipper, is what a total snob you are. Don't look at me like that. The only reason you give a shit about that woman is her tasting talent. And just because I want to use her to sell some product, that makes me a bad guy. What bullshit. Truth is, you hate me and anybody else who makes enough money to buy all the snooty overpriced wine we want, and not really give a shit what it tastes like. We can *afford* not to give a shit what it tastes like. You get that? And you, you pathetic weirdo, you'd put it in a museum or a temple somewhere and worship it. Well, we're just gonna drink it—maybe with a burger, maybe right out of the bottle—as a special 'fuck you' to people like you." He shook his head, squinting. "We might be philistines, but we're rich philistines who don't give a fuck about you or your wine."

Rage rolled through Brewster's brain, wave after wave, ordering him to punch his brother's sneering face. Somehow, though, his limbs were not getting the message. With a huge effort, he stayed on his feet. "You. You really...are...an asshole."

Through his wooziness, Brewster noticed Jock was standing very still, blinking furiously, looking puzzled, as if he were trying to remember something. His jaw worked spasmodically for a moment. "Wack," he said, finally. "Wack. Wack."

Brewster collapsed into a chair, smiling weakly. "Oh. That is beautiful. Say it again. Please. Like music."

"Wack. Wack, wack. Waaaaaaaaaaaaaack."

AT THE GRAVY STAIN

Fabrice double-parked, as usual, in front of the Multishots offices. The lobby was deserted. He took the elevator up to Nadia's fourth floor office, knocking softly before opening the door. She was on the phone, speaking in Russian.

Putting her hand over the receiver, she gestured for him to come in and sit down. "So sorry, *pupchin*, a moment please." Then she was back to her phone conversation, which lasted five minutes longer. When she hung up, she immediately began punching buttons, placing another call.

Fabrice was nervous and impatient. "*Chérie*, I know you are busy, but we do not want to make Margot wait for us, do we? It eez a bad impression, starting on zee wrong leg."

"I know, but I must do this now. Is no way around," she said, just before pouring a torrent of Russian into the phone, tapping her pen point on the desk for emphasis. She was only talking to her housekeeper, arranging to have dry cleaning picked up and reviewing the grocery list, but it all had the desired effect: delaying their departure.

The Bat slowed as she approached the restaurant parking lot; she saw Margot turn in, then lost sight of her as the Peugeot moved into a lane between rows of cars. No need

191

to crowd her if she was having a night out. Turning into the lot, the Bat eased to the right, following Margot. Chewing her bubble gum ferociously, she muttered, "If there's a line for the girls' room, somebody's gonna get hurt, swear to God."

It was when she turned down one of the lanes that she saw the parked Peugeot; she couldn't see Margot well because two no-neck guys were crowding around her. They were clearly not giving her hugs. A third man—swarthy, wrap-around sunglasses, bald—stood near the open rear doors of a green van parked in the middle of the lane, in the Bat's path. Margot was scuffling now, and shouting.

"Get the—! Don't touch me! Help!"

The Bat screeched up behind the van and flew out of her car, spitting her bubblegum as she went. She saw Margot apply one of her size ten sensible heels to the foot of the shortest and heaviest of the two; then, as he bent forward, she caught him on the temple with her elbow. He fell backwards, stunned. The second man punched Margot in the face, sending her reeling into the side of the Peugeot. He got duct tape on her mouth just as the first man, back on his feet, helped in the effort to drag her, struggling, to the van.

Margot later described the events as dreamlike. "Seems like it was over before I really knew what was happening. It was kind of like a ballet, but with some serious punchin'," she said later. "Those shitheads got blood on my nice white pants."

The Bat was in the air in seconds. The man near the van raised his arms to protect himself, but she delivered a lightning flying sidekick to the throat that sent him to the ground, writhing in agony. She whirled left to face one of the others who came at her and swung a huge right fist that made only glancing contact, the Bat having pulled away, shifting her weight to a backstance. With him momentarily off balance, she administered a knee strike that bent his lower left leg at a very unnatural angle. He screamed and bent toward her, after which she grabbed him behind the neck with both hands and brought his throat down abruptly on her raised knee. He crumpled, moaning. The heaviest of the three took his arms from around Margot and produced a gun from his waistband. He aimed at the Bat and fired, but not before Margot pushed his arm aside. In the second before he regained his footing, the Bat was on him, blocking his right arm and giving him a fist strike to the groin, which went slightly wide. This gave him a chance to lean into a punch with his left, one that was meant for her chin but that she drew away from, causing it to hit her solidly on the shoulder. She spun with the blow, to her left, coming around in a pure fury and, as he lurched forward, caught him with an elbow strike to the temple. He staggered away from Margot without dropping the gun, but could not recover fast enough to escape the Bat's final move, a ridge hand strike, tomahawk-like, to the carotid artery. The gun hit the ground just a second before he did. He lay almost still, grunting and wheezing.

The Bat scooped up the handgun and handed it to a dazed Margot. "Hang onto this for a sec," she panted. "Are you okay?"

Margot grimaced as she pulled the blood-spattered tape off her mouth. "That guy's not giving up," she said, gesturing toward the van and the first man the Bat had taken down. He was back on his feet and hunching toward the van's open rear doors. The Bat pivoted, took two steps and launched herself into a flying kick that landed on the back of his neck as his palms reached for the floor of the van. It produced an audible crack as he fell, head slamming against the bumper, then hitting the ground.

She turned back to Margot, catching her breath, gesturing at the gun. "Can you use that sucker if you need to?"

Wiping blood from her nose, Margot said, "Never fired one before. Why don't you take it?"

"I gotta take a wicked piss, is why," said the Bat, checking the Glock 17 and handing it back to her. "Aim and squeeze the trigger, that's all you gotta do. These fuckers'll respect you in the morning. I'll get the restaurant to call the cops."

"That phone Brewster gave me is right on the front seat."

'Yeah, but the crapper's in the restaurant. You don't want me pissin' in your Poogeot. Be right back."

Just then two police cruisers screeched into the lot, lights flashing. The restaurant hostess had called them as soon as the two "drunks" got belligerent just inside the entrance. The Bat told the cops she would be with them in a minute, after she took care of some urgent business. "Save the fuckin' world, but piss my pants! Isn't that the way it works, hah?"

The Bat made it to the restroom, but only after dazzling onlookers in the dining room with a few well-placed punches that quieted the troublemakers. They put up little resistance, surprised as they were to confront a short, wild-eyed woman wearing a bad mood and martial arts togs with a sizeable wet spot in the crotch. "These big jerkoffs always got the reach on me, but they're slow as shit," she explained to the stupefied hostess.

When the Bat emerged from the restaurant, the police had cuffed the three would-be kidnappers and seated them in the back of the squad cars. She saw the bloodied, vacant face of one of the attackers, staring out the back seat window, and charged over to it. She leaned down and sneered at him. He turned and faced forward. "Lookit me, ya douchebag! How'd that work out for ya? Hah? Maybe you should splash some shitty vodka on your face—you'll still be ugly, but it might stop the bleedin'."

"Anything's better than drinkin' it," called Margot, who was standing with two policemen, nursing her nosebleed and answering questions. She insisted she had no idea why the men would want to do it, but said they definitely wanted to abduct her; when the police saw tape rolls and a burlap bag on the ground, along with newspaper photos of her in the thugs' van, they were charged with assault and attempted kidnapping.

The Bat joined them. "It's gotta be the vodka crowd, pulling this shit. You gotta tell 'em the story. Go on. Tell 'em about Boy-tits."

"Boy-tits?" Margot looked confused.

They all looked up as Fabrice's BMW pulled into a parking space behind one of the police cruisers. An officer tried to wave him away, but Fabrice was out of the car in an instant, a mask of fear and confusion on his face. "I must see my friend, my great friend Margot! Margot, *chérie*! What has happened? You are all right?" He joined the group, gesturing passionately as he began to explain the dinner that he had scheduled with Margot, the great business opportunities that she would be hearing about. His explanation was interrupted by the revving of a car engine and the squeal of tires. Nadia had commandeered the BMW, taking off up 13th Street toward Market.

Though one of the officers called in an APB on the BMW and the very tall, slender Russian woman driving it, Nadia managed to get quickly to the Royal Lasuen Hotel on 9th Street, where the night manager, an old friend of hers, accepted her explanation that she was leaving the car in the underground garage for an associate who would come for it in the morning. She took a cab to the airport just in time for her flight to L.A., and, after buying some luggage and a few outfits at the airport, caught her scheduled flight to Moscow. There would be no return trip.

THE FATEFUL CHEEZOW

Brewster smiled and laid his head gently on the table. It had been an unauthorized operation, true. But even if it had left him strangely tired, he had performed well. He listened as Jock's quacking became more frantic, interspersed with muttering and an occasional puppy-like whimper. Was there nothing intelligible coming out of his mouth, or were Brewster's ears too relaxed to hear?

It was 2 a.m. before he stirred. All the cellar lights were on, but Jock was nowhere to be seen. He felt strangely light, not quite occupying his body. Had Jock slipped him something? It was the only explanation. But why? His first instinct was to get upstairs and call Dion. He needed to hear from the Bat, too. On rubbery legs, he made his way upstairs. There wasn't a sound in the house. He figured Corinne had been given a day off since Mum was in Carmel. Even if not, he decided not to invade her domain, the two rooms behind the kitchen she had occupied forever.

After calling out to Jock, Brewster saw a thin, pale stripe of light under the door to the study. That was how he discovered the body of his brother, collapsed on the floor, hands and lips covered with bright orange coloring. It was determined by investigators that Jock had retreated to the study, where he sat sobbing for some time (moist tissues on the floor around the body), drinking the better part of a bottle of cognac and gorging on a 16-ounce economy-size bag of Cheezows. Preliminary cause of death was listed as choking/asphyxiation, from a large piece of snack food lodged in his esophagus.

Because of the strange circumstances of Jock's passing, Brewster could not object to the medical examiner taking the body to the morgue for an autopsy. Ironic that with Jock dead, it was even more likely that they would detect Brewster's handiwork than had he remained alive. With whatever testing of blood and tissue they did, how could they miss components of Zipp and MLII? But would the examiner posit that he had been dosed, or that he had simply ingested a cocktail of drugs on the way to that bottle of cognac?

He was questioned at length by two SFPD officers who seemed to be equal parts amiability and suspicion. They told him he needed to be available for further questioning in the next few days, and Brewster reassured them as best he could, standing in the hallway, blanched, nervous, and sweaty. He decided he would wait until morning—which wasn't far off—before calling Mum and trying to contact Carolyn. Mum would be better off having had a cup of coffee and her first cigarette of the day before receiving the shocking news, and he wanted to locate Carolyn for a face-time visit rather than tell her over the phone, and— let's face it—he was interested in the floppy disks. Guilt and remorse swept over him in spite of everything that had passed between him and Jock, which only made him disgusted with himself. Why wasn't he contemptuous of his brother, triumphant in having dosed him? He certainly wasn't. All he could hear was Bernadette's carpy voice: Where's your spine, Brewster? Your killer instinct? Did I marry a boneless chicken breast?

Though it was after five o'clock, he decided to call the Bat. She was at Margot's place, sitting with her, decompressing.

"Where the hell ya been?" she demanded.

He told her Jock was dead.

"You're fuckin' with me."

He recounted the story of the old Bordeaux and his suspicions of getting dosed with something or other. No mention of him dosing Jock, of course. He could hear her passing all of it on to Margot. "I'm not feeling too good about much of anything right now, you can imagine."

"Well lemme tell ya, you're gonna feel a shitload better when I give you the story about tonight's little rumble. Swear to God, it was like fuckin' West Side Story or somethin'."

All his remorse vaporized when she told him about events at the Gravy Stain.

"And your bro was a big part of it," she said.

"And so was I, in a way."

"Bet your ass."

"And the cops are going after Nadia?"

"Yeah. I dunno if they'll get her. She's a pretty slippery bitch. Our buddy Fabrice is in custody, but I don't know how much they can pin on him. He'll probably walk."

"Imagine my relief." He asked to speak to Margot.

"All I cad say is, those vodka scubsuckers were worse than I thought," she said. "I god a pretty swollen dose, so I won't be workin' for a weeg or so."

"Get some ice on it. I wish I was there to give you a hug."

"I dew I had somethin' to be grateful for, siddin' here."

"Now don't be like that, Margot."

"Well shid, you just keeb on drivin' your chiggens to the wrog market. What gan I say?"

"How about saying how much you appreciate me and lust after me?"

"I abbreciate you a lod, how 'bout that? But I'd abbreciate you lods more if you were oud of the vodka business."

"For the hundredth time, I am not *in* the vodka business. What I am is kind of in shock right now. But I'm coming around later to visit, and I'll bring you something good for lunch, from the Coup de Food. You think you'll be up to that?"

"Yeah, okay. Kidnab attempts always gib me an ab-betite. Are you geddin' somethin' for Heidi?"

"Absolutely, if she'd like. Tell her I need to settle up with her. And I've got something else I need to talk to her about."

"She says, 'if you're buyin', shid yes.'"

SIGNING OFF FROM THE PINK SOFA

Brewster finally collapsed onto a pink satin-covered knock-off Louis XIV sofa that Mum had insisted on putting in the library. He dialed Dion's number. He was a little wary, not having his voice distortion unit with him, but at this point? What the hell. When Dion answered, Brewster used the code line signifying a successful operation, with major qualifications.

"We're gonna boogie oogie oogie til we just can't boogie no more."

Dion came back with the counter code. "They call me Mellow Yellow, quite rightly."

Using lines from Donna Summer, Procul Harem, Wilson Pickett, and Jimmy Gilmer and the Fireballs, he explained about Jock's death, the attempted kidnapping of Margot, and the likely escape of Nadia, presumably back to Russia. His brain was a nasty cocktail of heady triumph and cruel disappointment. He was facing a new world now, and, though many of its realities had yet to sink in, he was clear on one thing: Both he and the League were at risk of being exposed. And soon.

Through precise use of Barry Manilow, Gladys Knight and the Pips, and Little Peggy March, he also told Dion that serious fallout was likely and imminent. The coroner's report would be completed within a few days, and from there it was just a matter of the SFPD connecting some dots, likely bringing in the FBI and Interpol. Maybe even the DEA. It meant that they would ransack Brewster's life. It meant that they would associate him with the League and very possibly with some of its members.

Brewster could only imagine what Dion was feeling as he delivered this message. Would the League disband? It was unthinkable.

His personal plans had yet to take shape, but they would be drastic. Thinking about all the forces that would have him in their crosshairs, he could not take a chance. He saw no way out for himself other than leaving the country, possibly permanently. And the damn Silver Tinkle vodka would still be produced anyway, he thought angrily, even if he could manage to find Carolyn and get the disks from her. It was a bitter pill.

It is crucial to note here that Brewster, along with everyone else, assumed Nadia had fled with copies of the Silver Tinkle formula, as a hedge against any unforeseen problems. And indeed she had. Or thought she had. Once in Moscow, she conferred with microbiologists who had advised her previously and found that Jock had given her a disk that contained gobbledy-gook. Impressive-looking plant biology and chemical formulas that described several processes for hybridizing stone fruits. Enraged further by not being able to contact Jock, she met with silence from the Riga facility as well. The Latvians had somehow learned of Jock's death before Nadia, and assumed that their American connection was gone. With nationalist sentiment running high following years of demonstrations, and Latvia's independence only weeks away, they refused to agree to an exclusive partnership with an historic occupier/bully nation that was generally hated by their people. They of course had the formula for the vodka, and were defiant in refusing to give it up.

Both Brewster and Dion were silent for a moment as they realized the pivotal moment they had reached. Brewster felt the need to ask Dion to forgive him, and said: "Drove my Chevy to the levee, but the levee was dry."

Dion responded slowly, sounding positively genial: "As I walk through this world, nothing can stop the Duke of Earl." It was a great relief for Brewster to hear such a powerful line of code, signifying Dion's willingness to accept whatever fallout might result from the action against Jock. The message was, essentially—Don't worry. Take care of yourself.

Dion went on to tell him—with lines from the Carpenters, The Captain and Tennille, and The Four Tops—that a team of League agents had already blown up two warehouses in Riga containing the bulk of the new vodka, and were on track to torch the modified Russian wheat fields. They had not as yet been able to penetrate the robust security that surrounded the lab and distillery there. He said those efforts were ongoing.

Just before ending the call, Dion recited another powerful line, one that caused a surge of emotion in Brewster. It told him that, despite his League suspension, there would be further communication, somehow:

"Watch that scene, dig it, the Dancing Queen."

Feeling a sob rising in his chest, Brewster signed off with the most appreciative, warm, farewell code line:

"The name of the place is, I like it like that."

He felt a weight lift from him. He sat for a few minutes, as the light became stronger in the library, spreading slanted stained-glass patterns on the faded Sivas rugs that had been there for as long as he could remember. He cradled the phone in his lap, staring at the floor, exhausted. After a moment, he shook his head and stood. He needed to think about getting over to Margot's to have a serious talk with her and the Bat. He needed to explain, but how much could he say, really, without talking about the League? Then he thought: What to get for lunch from the Coup de Food? And: what would they be drinking?

THE LAST TAKE-OUT

Sitting in the mini-Cooper outside the Coup de Food, he called Mum. She didn't believe Jock was dead. Brewster must be lying. Instead of expressing grief, she accused him of not being supportive enough of Jock. Nor of her. Had he contacted Carolyn? He felt a roman candle ignite in his head and found himself spewing sparks into the phone. There are no reliable reports of the actual statements he made, but given "Nipper's" history in the family, one can imagine. Mum later would say only that he was upset and exhausted, and not himself. The call lasted barely more than five minutes. When he hung up it was as if he'd been underwater, and his grateful lungs were filling with air as he hit the surface.

Still in shock, he shuffled into the restaurant, greeted the staff, and settled in at the bar with a double cappuccino, extra chocolate. He realized he had no business indulging himself at a time when events might run him over like a truck, but he was feeling stubborn and defiant. He wasn't going to be arrested for Jock's murder, he felt certain of that; and it would take the SFPD at least a few days to connect the results of the autopsy to the League—and to him. He himself wasn't going to get any food down, but putting together a takeout order for Margot and the Bat helped focus him. *Mousselines de brochet* for Margot, she would like that. And for the Bat there was no doubt: *steak-frites*. He sipped his cappuccino. He felt nothing now for Jock, nothing for Mum. How could he be such a heartless bastard? Easily. Why hadn't he cut the straps off the strait-jacket long before this?

The churning queasiness he felt now had to do only with Margot, the League, and his future. *Only*? What he really wanted, to help him navigate all this, was a big snifter of Louis XIX cognac. But he let that thought go.

On the sidewalk in front of Margot's place, there were a couple of news camera crews, and a small group of reporters. As he mounted the steps to her door, he identified himself and said that Ms. Sipski would have a prepared statement for them at 5 p.m.

Margot buzzed him in, ice pack on her swollen sausage of a nose. "The dab phode has been riggin' off the hook," she said. "Bust be reporters."

Brewster said nothing, but handed off the food to the Bat and gave Margot a bear hug. The ice pack made it awkward. "Are you all right?" he asked, trying to keep the quaver out of his voice. "Don't worry about the reporters. How are you feeling?" He put his hands on her shoulders and peered into her eyes. "You probably should be lying down."

"Fug that," she spat. "I'b pissed." She regarded Brewster silently for a moment. Then she began to sob. Deep, racking sobs, as she leaned into his shoulder.

Startled, and beginning to tear up himself, Brewster said softly, "Oh, Margot. You are such a lovely person."

"And you're—you're pretty dab w—wonderful, too, Brewster." Ice pack in one hand, she managed to get her right arm around his neck, holding him tightly as she continued to sob. Brewster was lost in the sensation of her body against him, her hair against his cheek.

The Bat looked on for a moment, a small, goony smile on her face. She went to Margot's desk and turned off the ringer on the phone, so they now heard only the click and clatter of the answering machine. Then she slowly unpacked the food on the tasting table. As Margot's sobs subsided and Brewster wordlessly offered her his handkerchief, the Bat cleared her throat. "So! Anybody feel like some food? Hah?"

Suddenly self-conscious, Margot moved away from Brewster, dabbing her eyes to save what was left of her eyeliner. "I think I could ead somethin'." The charged atmosphere slowly melted away as they sat down.

"I don't want to keep you from your meal, but I'd like to hear all the details about the Gravy Stain," said Brewster, trying to be all business. "I told them outside that you'd issue a prepared statement at five."

Margot eyed him. "You wriding it? The stadement?"

"I think it's best, don't you? But we'll go over it together, what we should say."

She grunted. "As log as we kig Univod's ass, I'm habby."

"Great steak, Brew," said the Bat. "And thanks for not getting me any of that weird fish cake shit, no offense. I mean, I'm sure it's great and everything."

"Heidi, it'd be hard for you to offend either one of us at this point, I think that's safe to say," said Brewster.

"Aben to that," said Margot.

"So lunch isn't comin' outta my check, right? It's good as hell, but it tastes better on your tab, ya know? This fancy Bordeaux is the pooch's nuts, too."

Brewster watched them eat and sipped a glass of the white Graves, 1986 Domaine de Caguer, that Margot had opened for herself. Just what he needed to balance out the cappuccino and bring him down from the jagged, emotional moment with Margot. As he listened to the Bat recap some of the events at the Gravy Stain and note the pros and cons of the whole affair for her business (great for attracting new clients, but a little too high profile for her comfort), Brewster made a decision.

"This looks like the moment of truth for me, you guys," he said gravely, when there was a lull in the conversation and the Bat finished up her steak. He looked from Margot to the Bat and back again.

"What the hell do you bean?" said Margot, fork in one hand, ice pack in the other.

"I mean I haven't told you guys the whole story about myself."

Margot sniffed. "Like this is dews?"

"Now don't be like that. This is really difficult for me." And he proceeded to tell them about his double life with the League, about Univod, his suspension, about dosing his own brother. Everything.

WHAT MAYBE HAPPENED

It was a bombshell that left a crater of silence in the room. The Bat was the first to speak.

"So the deal is, you think you'll leave the country?"

"I don't think I've got much choice."

"Pretty harsh, Brew. Very tough. But if you gotta go, I can probably help with some of the—what'll we call 'em? Details?" She smiled grimly.

"I was hoping you'd say that. I'm really going to need some of your magic. Could I come around to your office tomorrow morning at around ten, say?

"No sweat. You got it."

Though it was hard to focus, the three of them somehow hashed out the best language for Margot to adopt in her statement to the press. Sensing that Brewster and Margot needed some time, the Bat then declared that she'd had enough excitement for a day and a night, and headed home. As she closed the door behind her, the two were suddenly very aware of being alone together, sitting opposite each other at the table where they had tasted so many wines.

"You're nod really leavin'." she said.

"I don't see any way around it. But you're going to stay here."

"Well, you bed I ab. I'b nod somebody who's gonna

follow you around, Brewster." Her indignation melted into pleading. "It's just nod who I ab! Can you see thad?"

He reached across the table and grasped her hand. "Of course I can. And you'll be much safer here than anywhere else, with the police aware that you're under threat, and with Heidi looking after you—which she will."

"Bud we'll see each other again sood, ride?" Her eyes searched his. "Ride?"

"Sure we will," he said, with a feeble smile. "You'll see. We'll make it happen."

We know Brewster met the Bat the following morning at his office to write her a check, thank her again, and tie up certain unspecified "loose ends." She swears there was no kissing on the mouth. Though she certainly is, to this day, still in contact with Brewster, she denies it. In talking with me nearly a year later, she insisted that Brewster told her nothing other than that he had made financial arrangements for himself and planned to be gone within 48 hours. It is noteworthy that she was the only person in his life who had the resources and connections to get him a Canadian passport or other good quality forged traveling documents. This is not a new observation; it was made often by law enforcement in the course of many interviews with the Bat, conducted by the SFPD, the FBI, and Interpol. Through it all, she stuck to her story.

"I dunno what these nimrods think they're gonna get from me. I'm a local PI tryin' to make a livin', for Chrissake! I don't have time for shit like they're talkin' about. Buncha assholes, you ask me."

For two months after Brewster's departure, Margot kept to herself. She granted few interviews. Occasionally, she had dinner with the Bat, with her friend Mitzy Quoff, or with a new friend, Dimitra "Doomie" Nastaca, a Romanian national who worked at the consulate in the city and had met Margot at one of her tasting presentations.

Margot was questioned more than a few times by law enforcement in San Francisco, about both the kidnap attempt and about Brewster. She was laconic through it all, explaining that the trauma to her nose had affected her psychologically, and she needed time and space to recover. In November she took up her work again, though it was apparent to many that her heart wasn't in it. It was burdensome to keep up the business end of her work, the endorsement contracts, the financial details of tasting events, things that Brewster had managed so well. More and more frequently at tasting presentations, too, the organizers would try to trip her up using the same old tired methods she had seen before: giving her wines they had blended beforehand, combinations of French wines and those from other countries —even sometimes tossing in bits of various liquors—all in hopes of generating the ultimate publicity coup, to have gotten the best of the great champion wine taster.

She called them out every time. But she was depressed.

In retrospect, it is possible she simply missed Brewster. For whatever reason, however, in March of 1992 she cancelled all her commitments and disappeared, much as had Brewster. Suspicions about how she accomplished such a clean escape fell again on the Bat, but she had the same response as always: a shrug. No amount of search and surveillance by any agency, public or private, ever yielded anything even vaguely incriminating.

But what was the fate of the League itself? It is strange

to have to admit that at that time I didn't have a clear answer. The reason is: I resigned. It was very painful, after so many years as an operative; but at an emergency meeting at the Control Hub two days after Brewster's last call to Dion, a meeting which included all members except the three who had been tasked with the sabotage operations in Latvia and Russia, the discussion centered on which of us were too clearly at risk of compromising the League because of frequent operational contact with Brewster. I was a prime candidate, having met with him during field operations dozens of times, in Reno, London, Beaune, Cuernavaca, Lyons, Honolulu, Des Moines, and other venues. Any security camera footage or eyewitness testimony from those venues might serve to unravel the identities of everyone in the League, so to protect the others I felt it was my duty to resign my position, horrible though that was. I should note that I made the decision on my own; I was not pressured by Dion, Hideo, or anyone else. Okay, maybe a little by Impnitz, but that was to be expected. In the event, five other operatives resigned with me, for the same reason.

Because my last direct contact with the League dates from that afternoon in 1991, for many months I had no better information than anyone else about its fate. Which is what I insisted in statements to every branch of law enforcement you know about, plus a couple you have certainly never heard of. I was in mourning for this gallant organization and its noble goals. I found myself wanting to call Dion's direct line, and Hideo's, too, hoping they would answer; but I never did, of course, for fear of alerting law enforcement.

If Brewster's worst moment came when he realized Margot had discovered his connection to Spodie

International and Isopropov vodka, mine was in leaving the League—dropping off a cliff into nothingness, distraught that my comrades had likely disbanded the organization. I was shadowed by the police for a while. They were sure I had information they could use, but I ignored them as much as possible as I went about the business of rebuilding a shattered life.

I took a job with Transcontinental Corporate Family Vineyards, just to pay the bills. It was soul-killing, yes, but kind of like bleeding to death—soothingly gradual its effects. I worked as a manager in human resources, fielding a steady stream of sexual harassment charges and mollifying prickly, vain winemakers complaining about insubordination from the large numbers of employees who despised them. I started out barely willing to drink the bad coffee in the lounge and ended up using non-dairy creamer and gorging on dry, two-day-old chocolate donuts crusted with colored sprinkles. Even for a lover of coffee shop fare, this was sheer self-abasement. I recount the depths to which I sank only to contrast them with the jolt of excitement I felt when, one morning in January of 1993, there was news. News of the League.

A group of coworkers had gathered around the computer screen of a fellow HR manager, talking excitedly. Nothing unusual, since we were all new to the internet and to computers in general, and a new tech revelation—one that just had to be shared—seemed to come along every day. It was when I caught the word "quack," repeated over and over, that I decided to investigate. My blood surged wildly, like a tide against a seawall, when I saw what they were looking at. It was a news article from the previous day's Washington Courier-Sanitizer, describing the scene as Byron Balltower, CEO of Liquid Incrapescence, makers of the popular rum, "Gut Check," was rendered unable to deliver the keynote speech to Guilt Marketers of America because of an uncontrollable fit of "quacking." The article speculated on possible causes, but focused most of its attention on the "anonymous group" who had carried out similar chemical attacks in prior years.

It hit me like a shot of electrical current. Looking at that computer screen, I felt like the last human being alive, receiving communication signals from deep space. At first I told myself it didn't matter whether I would ever make contact with the group, but of course I was lying. I wanted to get back in the saddle and punish some of the industry scumsuckers and shitbags who kept popping up like turds in the industry punch bowl. But as my head cleared, I realized I had no way to contact any of the team—if it actually was the remnants of the League—and didn't even know how to begin a search. So I did the next best thing: I quit my job and moved to New Zealand. It was a personal response to the League's resurgence, as if I had just snapped out of a hypnotic state. It was an expression of freedom, mental and emotional shackles clattering to the ground. I have never regretted the move; it is a beautiful country with stately scenery, wonderful people, and spectacular variations on my favorite coffee shop foods.

Strange to consider that in that moment of liberation, as I silently thanked the League—and Brewster—for their inspiration, Brewster had already been in contact with the new League. Months before, in fact. He had also fought the mightiest battle of his life, against all-too-familiar enemies.

TRACKING MARGOT, 2ND EDITION

For a decade, I have kept an electronic scrapbook of the new League's accomplishments, crowing over each one, as if I had been involved. Maybe the operations were less frequent and smaller scale than the events chronicled in this book, but they're still impressive as hell. Who didn't love seeing the take-down of such full-on Shitheads as Quim Bunkers, the Dutch cheese magnate who spent years "hunting" big game in Africa with hand grenades, and who puts an inlay of real elephant tusk in the cap of every bottle of his "Grenade" brand gin. "Pull the pin on great taste!" said the ads.

My ass.

They also managed to dose the brothers Shaleze and Bukram Nosairs, who produced the "Nice and Friendly" label of Canadian whiskey, which contained partially de-salinated seawater cut with invert sugar, "natural flavors," and street-quality primate dopamine. It was especially exciting that the New League apparently deployed some cutting-edge, new ordnance in that operation. Reports of the incident, at a political fundraiser, describe the brothers as compulsively goosing anyone in the immediate environs while singing a variety of Verdi arias. They broke down in uncontrollable sobs at irregular intervals, which made me think the weapon in question was a new generation of MLII. In any case: Bravissimo.

My joy would have been complete if they had eventually managed to wreak havoc in Russia, in light of everything Jock Hotte and Nadia Scrotova had done. It stuck in my craw that persistent industry rumors told of Nadia landing on her feet with Univod, finessing her renegade Silver Tinkle conspiracy and insinuating herself back into its good graces. There were more than a few times it seemed the League might have dosed Yeltsin with MLII; given his emotional outbursts, his shouting and weeping, it was hard to tell. But I knew it wasn't true, any more than it would be likely they could dose Vladimir Putin today. Too many security hurdles. And, as I mentioned already, he's a dry drunk, anyway.

As soon as I saw that first news story about what I was sure was the new League, I called the Bat, just to suggest to her that, in case she ever happened to hear from Brewster or Margot, she should let them know: the League Lives!

"Hey, Vinnie, what am I, a customer service call center?" she said. "It's like I told the FBI douche bags, if you want to find Brew, you're going to have to pull up your panties and do it yourself. I got a business to run here. Look, gimme your number and I'll call ya if I hear anything. I hope you're havin' a good time in New Zealand—just stay away from all those horny sheep, 'kay?"

A discouraging exchange. But the next day, she called me from what she described as "an indisposed location." She said she never talked much on her office line anymore, because it was tapped. She also said she honestly couldn't tell me anything about Brewster's whereabouts.

"Can't or won't?" I asked her.

"Whatever. Smells the same when it drops in the bowl, hah?"

She did give me some inspiration, though. She told me that Brewster had somehow made contact with the remnants of the League the previous fall; she also gave me the phone number of Juliénas Morgon, Margot's old friend whom she stayed with for six months after leaving San Francisco. When I got her on the phone initially, Juliénas exercised the same precautions the Bat used; a few days later she called me from what sounded like a café or a restaurant, and talked for nearly an hour. It was she who told me the amazing story of Margot's final confrontation with Univod, and Brewster's role in it.

In her typical head-on fashion, Margot had apparently bolted to Bucharest in March of 1992, with only a small suitcase and an artfully forged passport to supply her with an assumed name. Her new persona included bleached hair and a minimum of her beloved eyeliner. She was thinking big, and fearlessly. To her, Romania was not just a new frontier for her wine explorations, but one of the front lines in the battle against Univod and vodka itself. President Nicolae Ceausescu had been a Univod man for decades, but his execution in 1989 had broken its stranglehold and opened the door for the huge number of small producers of slivovitz, the reasonably famous plum brandy, to form partnerships and coops to market their products more aggressively. She saw the situation as a golden opportunity to improve the general quality of slivovitz and make inroads into Univod's share of the spirits market, not just in Romania, but potentially in other, now unchained, Eastern European countries.

It turned out to be tough going, even with the affable young guide and translator provided to her by the new and distinctly pro-European directorship of the Transylvanian Ethanol Gild. Because of inflation and austerity measures put in place by newly-elected president Ion Iliescu, money was too scarce to allow for much investment in equipment and marketing. Worse still, impoverished citizens were getting shit-faced in droves on the cheap vodka that then flooded Eastern European nations, courtesy of Univod. That bit of information kept Margot's temper at a constant simmer.

Her real problem, though—a perfect Catch 22—was name recognition. Slivovitz producers were not coming to meet with the fictitious name on her passport, but with Margot Sipski, the famous expert taster whose exploits, though less known in Romania, were being loudly celebrated by the Ethanol Gild. As the size of the groups grew, the more her presence as Margot Sipski was trumpeted in local media. It was inevitable that she would become concerned for her safety. During the day, she would dismiss her fears as paranoia: she was too small a fish to matter in the wide ocean of vodka. Still, she would sometimes wake in the black of night, heart thumping, wondering if Univod had located her and had her squarely in its cross-hairs.

Using my favorite form of cheap wisdom, retrospect, it is not surprising that Nadia Scrotova herself, ensconced in a Kremlin office as a Univod senior vice president, was indeed interested in, not to say obsessed with, her whereabouts. Still smarting from the botched kidnapping and Margot's continued public rage against vodka, she was powerfully, coldly focused on revenge. While Margot was still in California, Nadia thought better of any attempt to harm her; the media spotlight was too bright, and there just weren't enough other feasible suspects. Any action could easily become a PR nightmare for Univod. But when word of Margot's disappearance from San Francisco reached her, she immediately saw to it that Univod's intel bloodhounds were unleashed. Would they have located her without a little help from Michael Jackson? It's a moot question now.

The famous 1992 Bucharest concert had been a surprise when it was announced months before, but Margot, not particularly a fan, hardly registered it except to be amused by the antics of amped-up young Romanians suddenly sporting a ton of Michael Jackson gear. What she had not considered was the media swarm. In the two weeks prior to the October 1st concert date, waves of reporters and stringers descended on Bucharest like junkies looking for a fix: local color, sidebar features, fresh angles on anything even vaguely related to the concert. It didn't take long for them to discover a semi-famous American female wine expert living in Bucharest, whose current work was quirky and quixotic. The interviewers were relentless. She successfully dodged some, but not all. Yes, she knew Michael Jackson's music. Yes, some of it was pretty good. No, she had no plans to attend the concert. What am I doing here? Well, do you know anything about how great slivovitz can be? You should talk to some of these people. And do you guys know the truth about vodka?

She couldn't help herself.

It was when Margot's name and face appeared on the UBC international satellite channel, whose broadcast reach in the wake of the Soviet collapse included both Western and Eastern Europe, she realized she had likely blown what was left of her cover. Even a one-minute feature segment on the Umbilical Broadcasting Company News represented huge exposure. She called her friend Juliénas in Paris and asked if she had seen the news clip. She had not.

"I think I really messed up this time," she said ruefully. "*Que je suis conne!* But I'm not ready to panic. I'm gonna take a deep breath and keep workin', though like I told you before, there aren't many growers or distillers here who've got the scratch to make big changes. I did a tastin' at one place where they used Yosemite Sam shot glasses! I had to laugh. There's a bushel of enthusiasm here, but about a thimbleful of money."

"I will not even ask about this Sam person on the glasses. But Margot, you must watch for your own safety. Why not leave there for a while? Until this publicity goes away?"

The answer was no.

THE CALL OF CACAO

When he fled San Francisco, Brewster was a marked man. International law enforcement had him on their Most Hated and Envied List, and Univod had teams of agents looking for him. ("Agents" might be too genteel a word—more like hired thugs and hit men.) Even with his new passport, he knew it was unwise to go to Europe; so he first chose Southeast Asian destinations where he could educate himself about tea and perhaps make a living growing it. But according to the sketchy sources we have, which include Juliénas Morgon and contacts made from following up on her suggestions, Brewster made that choice more from panic than from actual desire. He visited Ceylon and Malaysia, where he spent nearly three months exploring possibilities in the Cameron Highlands, but I believe he knew deep down where his real destiny lay.

Chocolate.

Are all the stories true? Certainly some are apocryphal, but we have a rough outline of what happened. In early 1992, Brewster had taken up residence in Chuao, Venezuela, and had begun exploring the culture and tradition of growing cacao. By mid-summer, he had begun touring the surrounding region for possible planting sites and had met the legendary old *brujo*, Don Fungibo. It is believed that it was this shadowy figure who, deeply touched by Brewster's powerful enthusiasm and strange clothes, led him deep into the mountain jungles where unique old plantings of the cacao tree, *Theobroma cacao*, were growing. It was he who found loyal and discreet workers to revive the plantation, and provided Brewster with guidance on cultivation and processing of the beans. Brewster was a fast learner, and even his initial setbacks in cacao processing and blending experiments convinced him—and Don Fungibo—that eventually he would produce extraordinary, world-class chocolate.

But in late September of '92, for once, the big news in Brewster's life had nothing to do with chocolate. It was about Margot's TV appearance. On the day after her interview, he was in his office as usual, watching the UBC satellite news and enjoying a lunch of a couple of tostada-like Reina Pepiadas, washed down with a 1990 white Montagny. One minute he was watching a sweet, grandmotherly type brandishing a Braun kitchen gadget, and the next it was a tight shot of a bleach-blonde, eyeliner-deprived Margot, wearing her usual wry smile as she talked about Michael Jackson and—ye gods—vodka.

He nearly gagged on a big swallow of Montagny. Shocked and elated to see her face, he was equally furious that she was still carrying on about the evils of vodka. On international television, no less. Oh yes, he thought, nodding grimly, she was at least that stubborn. He talked to the TV then—shouted at it actually—telling her how beautiful she looked, and would she please get her goddam head back down in the foxhole?

He called the Ethanol Gild in Bucharest, leaving an

after-hours message for Margot to call him the next evening, at a café in Caracas. He had sworn he would not give away his precise location for anything, and there were a couple of places in Caracas that had been serving as communication points. It was a terrible drive from Chuao, but if he left very early, he could be there before noon.

When he finally spoke with her, it was with one hand pressed against his free ear to reduce the din of the lunchtime rush.

"Hey, Brewster. Did you join the Latino foreign legion or what?"

"Margot? Hello? My God but it's good to hear your voice!"

"Yeah, great to hear from you, too. Uh, listen, just to cut to the chase, I think I got a bucket of trouble here."

"I'm not going to ask about Bucharest or what you think you're accomplishing, Margot, but I can tell you right now that the best thing you could—"

"You mind if I tell you how this looks to *me*? Would that be okay with you, do ya think?" He could hear the heat flow into her voice.

He took a deep breath. "Sure, of course. Sorry. Please tell me."

"So here's the story: lots of people coming around askin' for me this mornin'. Office people here said a bunch of 'em don't have press credentials. I was gonna tough this out and stay around longer, but I realized this mornin' that I'm way over my head. I don't like the way any of it's goin', so I'm headin' for Paris."

"But you should come down to Caracas! The farther away you get the better, doesn't that make sense?"

She sighed. "There you go, Brewster. We're on the phone one entire minute and you start in tellin' me how to put cream in my coffee. *Plus ça change*, huh?"

"But are you really figuring they suddenly won't care anymore, after that UBC segment? They'll just forget about you if you leave Romania? Is that realistic?"

"You know, I'm just happy as hell to hear from you, and so happy that you're wearin' your nice fascist dictator pants and everythin', but what *I* want is to go back to Paris. It's where I'm comfortable, Brewster. I am pretty shaky right now, and I need to get some happy under my belt. Eat some good food, drink some good wine. I heard they're havin' a weird warm spell there, too, so I can sit out on a café terrace all afternoon if I like. And I wanna see Juliénas, of course. I'm gonna take a day to get the Gild people up to speed with my projects, though. I don't want all my work to fall into some bottomless file cabinet somewhere. But I'm gettin' to Paris right quick."

He gritted his teeth. "Listen, my dearest Margot. If you're looking for a place to be anonymous, does Paris— of all places—really fit that bill? You're a celebrity there, for God's sake."

"Don't hand me that! You saw me on the UBC clip. Would anybody recognize the Margot of even a year ago as that person? It'd be like recognizin' you if you had a tan."

"Okay. Okay, fine. Then I'll meet you there, as soon as I can get a flight. Don't go anywhere near Juliénas's place, okay? They've got to know about her, and if they *are* hunting for you, that's one place they'll be watching. I'm going to book a room at the Pauvrot, on the Boulevard Fauche— you know it?"

"I'm not stayin' in a room with you, Brewster, if that's what—"

"Oh right, of course," he said testily. "Two rooms. I'll get two rooms. What could I have been thinking?"

GOING IT ALONE

B rewster arrived in Paris a little more than forty hours after his phone conversation with Margot. After a layover in Washington, D.C. and a suffocatingly warm passenger cabin, his blue seersucker jacket and taupe pants were looking particularly lived-in. He was greeted by the freakish heat spell Margot had spoken about, the météo promising no less than 30 degrees Celsius for several days.

He arrived at the Pauvrot a little after 10 a.m., sweating heavily, wilted by air that seemed too heavy to enter his lungs and make it back out again. Like so many hotels in Paris, the Pauvrot was an older place, lovingly renovated within the constraints of available space, and Brewster appreciated the atmosphere: rickety elevator, narrow corridors with plush carpeting, tastefully appointed smallish rooms with an eclectic mix of belle epoch-style furniture. The mini-bars were standard—with standard outrageous prices—but the bathrooms were oversized, with lots of accent tile work.

Margot had not yet arrived, so he focused on arranging the room. Exactly what he did, and the account of everything that occurred on that extraordinary day, was, as I said, reported to me by Juliénas. Even so, I can't pretend not to have filled in some details myself—in the strictest spirit of journalistic alacrity, naturally.

Brewster worked as quickly as he could, still sweating though the air-conditioning was churning away. He realized just how anxious he was. Where was Margot? Shouldn't she have arrived first? Afraid he would miss her, he ordered lunch from room service, along with a bottle of champagne on ice and two flutes. The flutes went onto the shelf above the minibar, next to four (ugh) all-purpose wine glasses. He wolfed his *turbot* with chive *beurre mousseux*, washing it down with a half-bottle of simple Chablis. He didn't want to risk ordering anything too lavish, for the usual reason: he could be a danger to himself. He feared indulging too much and not being at his best when Margot—or trouble—arrived. Because he did expect trouble. If precautions proved unnecessary, that was one thing. But to be unprepared was unthinkable.

When everything was in place, he turned off the air-conditioning, removed the control knob from the thermostat, and opened the large casement windows. A rush of street noise and humid air engulfed him.

He flinched when the phone rang, a jarring noise in a small room. Two quick steps to the desk. He picked up the receiver slowly, dreading bad news.

"Allo?"

He heard a bright, bell-like baritone voice. "You can't roller skate in a buffalo herd."

Brewster's legs nearly gave out; he pivoted and dropped into the desk chair. His mind was blank for a moment, then racing. It was League code, of course: request for identification under emergency conditions. And it was Impnitz's ID. Brewster couldn't process it. *Impnitz*. Impnitz, who

227

had always seemed to hate him like Margot hated vodka. His thoughts were stuttering like a flustered suitor, but he remembered the correct response, his own ID under emergency conditions.

"I got the boogie-woogie like a knife in the back."

Brewster's heart was thumping in his ears as Impnitz told him, by way of The Zombies, Johnny Rivers, The Shirelles, Sonny and Cher, and Bobby Vinton, that there were only seven remaining League members, and that all but he were on assignment. He was alone in the new Control Hub, but Dion had instructed him to make contact with Brewster and offer help.

"Teen angel, can you see me?" Brewster had to ask how they had located him.

With crisp sequences from Judy Collins, The Iron Butterfly, Tiny Tim, and Roy Orbison, Impnitz told him that the League had a friend at the Transylvanian Ethanol Gild—but so did Univod, and it would be best to flee the Pauvrot for another hotel, or leave Paris entirely.

"Precious and few are the moments we two can share," Brewster said, telling Impnitz he could not leave without achieving his goal, which was of course meeting up with Margot. If he fled, she would not know where to look for him, and would be completely vulnerable.

Before signing off, Impnitz used lines from the Everly Brothers, The Boxtops, and The Hollywood Argyles to indicate he could come to Paris and provide backup, but would need 24 hours to do so.

"Sometimes when we touch, the honesty's too much," said Brewster, offering thanks, but signaling he would go it alone.

THE HEAT

Brewster sat in the desk chair, feeling like he would burst. Dion had found a way to carry on. The League wasn't dead. His sense of triumph and the excitement of seeing Margot again were held in check by dread of the very real threat that faced him now. Impnitz had spelled it out: Univod knew where he was and that Margot was to join him. Why was he hearing Bernadette's voice in his head at a moment like this, as annoying as the bleating of a large truck's backup warning? *Stop looking like such a victim. These things don't just happen to you, you know: you create them with your terrible attitude!* He was overwhelmed for just for a moment, numbed by a rush of emotion, the traffic noise, the humidity, the smell of car exhaust. Then his thoughts cleared.

At about 3:30 there was a frantic—or was it annoyed?—series of knocks on the door and a muffled version of Margot's voice. He swung the door open. For all her bleached hair and toned-down eyeliner, her pair of old jeans and a Madras shirt, it was the Margot he loved. He smiled warmly. "Margot."

"Hey, Brewster," she said gently. There was light in her eyes as she stood, stock still, in the doorway. "I'm gonna tell you up front: I missed you." She gave him a long hug, then a peck on the cheek. She smiled playfully. "Looks like you've gained a little weight." She patted his gentle paunch.

"I was kind of hoping for another kind of greeting," he answered, half wistful, half irritated. "Like a long, soulful look from you, and then something like, 'I knew you'd come.'"

"Well of course I knew you'd come. You told me on the phone, 'member? So are you gonna let me in, or just stand there blockin' the doorway? I dumped my bag in my room and figured I should check in with you right quick." She flopped into the desk chair. "Hoo-ee, I am beat! I thought it'd be safer to take a train to Sofia and fly from there, so that's what I did. You just get here?"

"A couple of hours ago. But listen, Margot, I have to tell you a few—"

Noticing the open window, she said, "It's pretty damn warm in here. Why isn't the air on? And what's with the window?" She smiled her wry smile. "You hopin' to lose some weight?"

He sighed heavily. Perching on the bed, he said, "You really need to hear a couple of things quickly." He told her about the call from Impnitz.

"Did ya bring a gun?"

"A gun? Are you kidding? Those things are dangerous!"

"My hero."

"I'm choosing to hear that minus the sarcasm. Look, I have a plan that might get us out of this if we stay put, but 'might' is the operative word. How do you feel about making a run for it? Right now."

"And go where?"

"I'm going to say Caracas, and you're going to object."

"Why not stay in Paris?"

"We could do that, yes, but why take the risk? I hate to repeat myself, but the farther away from all this we get, the better."

"I hate it when you repeat yourself, too. But why don't we just make it to another hotel, somewhere borin' like in the Seventh? Those guys won't find hide nor hair of us."

"Margot, I think you're out of your mind, but let's get to another hotel and then at least we'll be arguing somewhere relatively safe. It's very scary that we don't even know the shape of the threat."

It was at that moment that the shape of the threat became clear.

The door lock produced four or five loud clicks, which brought both of them to their feet. Two figures stepped into the room, silent and serious as funeral directors. Dark suits and unfashionably wide ties. The shorter and older of the two was slight but ramrod straight, with neatly-parted gray hair and soft, puppy-dog brown eyes. He was downright handsome. The fine jaw and broad forehead of a matinee idol. He had a handgun trained on them, one with an impressive-looking silencer. The taller one was younger, more sallow, belligerence showing in blue eyes crowded close around a sharp beak of a nose. He was chewing gum, but strangely languidly. He carried a suitcase.

Brewster moved instinctively, positioning himself in front of Margot, shielding her. "Don't worry about it, Brewster," she said. He knew she was trying to be blasé, but her voice wavered.

"Move away from the lady, please," said the shorter

man, in a droning voice which suggested a college lecturer. His accent was British but nasal, nothing very toffee. "Lovely, thank you. Now, normally you'd have been dispatched by now, to be quite candid. My associate and I are professionals, after all. But because our client—"

Brewster had weighed the situation: a third floor room, yes, but window open. Not enormously thick walls in these places, too. He decided it was worth it, and shouted, "*Au secours*! Help!" until the butt of the pistol came down on his head and he fell to the floor. The younger assassin snatched a roll of duct tape out of his suitcase and covered Brewster's mouth as he lay on his side, stunned. He then pivoted quickly, slamming the window shut.

Margot automatically moved toward Brewster, but the younger man bounded back and knocked her to the floor with a punch to her left temple. She groaned in spite of herself.

"Will you be requiring a bit of tape as well? No, I doubt it. You're a clever girl." said the older man, gesturing to his partner. "So tiresome, these faux heroics."

When both had been bound with tape at wrist and ankles, arms behind their backs, the younger intruder was out of breath. "Hot in here, init?" he said. They then noticed the control knob missing from the thermostat. The older man, irritated, said, "Bloody hell."

"You did see there's a bottle of cold champagne on the fridge, right?" the younger one said, trying to sound casual as he took off his jacket, revealing a holster that held his own weapon.

"Don't be daft. You've conveniently forgotten that we're not to eat or drink anything in this place. This bloke has a reputation, yeh?" He turned back to his prisoners, Margot seated in the desk chair, Brewster on the floor, his back up against a leg of the desk. "As I was saying—before your little spasm of courage—I have been instructed to offer you a deal, as follows: either we eliminate you both, toot sweet, or, alternate option, Ms. Sipski participates in a promotional video for vodka products after which we release Mr. Hotte." He gestured to his partner to pull the duct tape from Brewster's mouth.

ALCOHOL, CAMERA, ACTION!

While Brewster gasped for breath, Margot blurted out, "Like we're supposed to trust you people? I'd trust a damn bartender before I'd trust somebody like you."

"What happens to Margot in all this?" said Brewster.

"I regret that Ms. Sipski will perish in any case."

After a moment of stunned silence, Margot said in a small voice, "I'll do it."

"Don't, Margot! They'll kill us both, anyway!"

The older man planted himself in front of Brewster and placed the tip of the silencer on his forehead. "I beg your pardon. I phrased that part of the offer poorly. If Ms. Sipski does not agree to participate in the video, I am dispatching you forthwith."

"I told you I'd do it, are you deaf? Now back off!" A sob lodged in Margot's throat as she finished speaking.

Brewster was struggling and squirming. "Margot, no! They're not going to let me go, and you know it. I kind of like it this way—we go together. The death bond! If you do this, it'll be a huge gift to Nadia Scrotova. It's your whole damn life you're—"

"Shut up, Brewster. I'm doin' it. You guys get that? I'm doin' it, okay?"

He withdrew the gun barrel, looking satisfied.

"Excellent choice." He turned to his associate, gesturing with his chin toward the suitcase. "Let's get cracking, me lad." He stepped behind the prisoners to the desk phone and made a call. When he spoke, his voice was ingratiating, fawning. "Good afternoon. My God, you don't sound too chipper. Yes, fine. Ms. Sipski has accepted the terms. Yes. We're waiting for you. Perfect." He hung up.

"How about just a tad of that champagne before we get it all sorted out?" said the younger man. "Looks like a really posh bottle, that one."

"That," said Brewster with authority, "is a 1978 Swillinger Recently Engorged. A great wine."

There was an argument between the two assassins, which ended with the older man taping the prisoners' mouths and threatening his associate with his weapon. "Get to it. Now!" he snarled.

"Bugger it," said the younger man. "Bloody bottle isn't even open. But that's fine. I'll just get meself a drink of water, yeh? Objections to that?" He opened the minibar fridge.

The older man gave him a dark look. "Go ahead then. But make sure the seal is good. In fact, get me one as well, if there's two. I'm parched."

They took deep, audible swallows from their plastic bottles of Avion water, after which the younger man pulled a video camera from the suitcase and proceeded to don a shoulder mount. He was checking readings when they heard a single loud knock at the door. It was Nadia.

By all accounts, she looked distinctly unhealthy. Chalk-white face, huge dark glasses, lipstick spread slightly beyond her generous lips. She wore snug black kid leather pants, a scoop-neck seafoam green tunic, and her standard 5-inch heels. She was not happy.

"How was I so stupid?" she muttered, placing her large Gucci bag on the settee. "This best day in life, almost ruined by lack of discipline. So stupid." She forced a sickly smile as she turned to Brewster and Margot. "Ah, but to have both of you here, stupid bitch, is greatest joy for me. We will make movie together! Is wonderful. And idiot brother can be audience. Such a great day." She turned to the men. "Those bottles of water. You brought them with you?" When they shook their heads, she berated them until the older man explained that they checked the seals before drinking any. She calmed down. "Then you can give me some. My mouth is like sand. So hot in here. Is it me? No, not the bottle, you animal! Bring a glass, but rinse and wipe first. Hotte is idiot, but he learned cunning habits from his outlaw friends."

When Nadia had emptied her glass, the older man said, "Are you all right? What happened to you? If you don't mind my asking."

She waved her arm is disgust. "Was stupid. Playing drinking game called 'Your Cleavage or Your Life' with Gianni Versace and Anna Wintour. Very late. Too much vodka." Her tone became more commanding. "You will take the tape from Hotte's mouth now. So he can have his…medicine."

"Right," said the older man, setting his gun on the bed. "We're holding him in place then?" He gestured to the younger one, who knelt next to Brewster, smiling icily, grasping him behind the neck. Looking at Brewster, he said, "Ready for a treat, are we?"

Brewster twitched his head from side to side, eyes wide, full of anxiety. Whatever words he said were a muffled nothing. Nadia pulled something from her bag, then turned to face him with a look of triumph. She held up four candy bars in blue and red wrappers. "Cadbury Fruit and Nut, just for you, idiot brother! And you will eat all, believe me." She chuckled maliciously.

Brewster's roar was muted; he struggled, but could do nothing.

The older man unwrapped the bars and set them on the carpet. "Now, lad, when the tape comes off your mouth, you'll not shout, or I'll be forced to pistol whip your girlfriend. And I know you don't want that."

It was sad, horrible business. They held Brewster's nose and pushed the bars, one after another, past his teeth. He gagged, spit chunks on the floor, only to have them picked up and jammed back into his mouth. He moaned as he finally began to chew, his face a mask of disgust. He shivered with horror. "So repulsive," he wheezed, when he finally caught his breath. "Oh God."

They made a point of not wiping his face before the duct tape went back on.

Nadia then gestured toward Margot. "Has she seen the words she is to say for the camera?" The answer was no. She pulled a bottle out of her bag. "I can anyway first introduce her to her selected drink for this afternoon." With a nasty smile, she waved the bottle—Isopropov Silver Tinkle—in front of Margot. "This! This is what you will praise! This is what you will drink! A great movie plot, yes?"

ONE MORE DRINK, WITH FEELING

Under pressure, Margot turned out to be a terrible actress. Free of duct tape, she stood shakily, leaning against the desk, holding a glass of vodka like it was a dead rat. She couldn't manage anything that came within a hundred yards of a smile. "Hi. I'm Margot Sipski, ace, uh, ace wine and spirits expert, and I'm here with my, um, good friend, Nadia Scrotova, to tell you a little secret. Everybody—including me—makes mistakes. Nobody gets it right every time, that is unless you're talking about the folks who make the incredibly, uh, delicious Isopropov Silver Tinkle vodka. Mmmmm. So smooth, so luscious, so sophisticated, it'll make you a totally different person after just three glasses. With a flavor as big as—"

"What is this?" demanded Nadia. "Funeral? You sound like you took drugs! Again, pliz! More filling!"

It was at the beginning of the third take that the quacking began.

The older man began clearing his throat, first looking puzzled, then outraged as he dropped the large cards Margot had been reading from.

Margot looked first at Nadia, then at Brewster, who had little trouble keeping his face straight with such a big slice of duct tape across the middle of it.

Nadia's look of incomprehension quickly turned to panic. "What is it? What is wrong?" She clutched at her throat. "Oh God, the focking water!" She threw a blazing glance at Brewster. "You, you little shit!" Then, to the older assassin: "Kill him now, do it!"

By now, the younger man was quacking loudly and had plopped down on the floor where he had dropped the camera. The older man had tears in his eyes as he sat down gently on the bed. His face melted into a painful grimace as he began to weep. His quacking continued like hiccups.

"Kill him, I said!" screamed Nadia.

"No," he said softly. (Quack) "You don't understand." He picked up his gun and popped out the clip.

"Then I'll do it myself!" Nadia lunged to grab the clip, but the man made mewling noises and clutched it to him like a silent movie hero might hold his damsel. Tears poured down his face.

"This is (Quack) a bloody stupid display, especially from a beautiful soul like you, Nadia. You, (Quack) who I've loved from the moment I (Quack) saw you. So sad."

She went for the younger man's gun, still in its holster, but he shoved her hard enough to send her staggering. He held his chin up to keep the tears from falling. Addressing no one in particular, he said, "It's tragic, really. So sad. Just a few years ago. All I wanted, (Quack) the only thing I wanted, was to write adverts. Some clever things, plenty of (Quack) jokes. To sell Watney's or Tetley or some (Quack) kind of crisps. But no, they said. Even me mam, she said I wasn't good enough. (Quack) Never. But, they said, well, (Quack) you could be a wine critic (Quack) if you like. That's what Englishmen do." He shook his head ruefully.

"But who wants (Quack) that? Having to say shite like, 'a wine with great poise and (Quack) breeding. A lovely, foursquare mouthful.'" He shuddered. "Wankers. What a fate." He looked around, suddenly fierce. "So killing (Quack) seemed like the only path for me. And (quack) I'll not be blamed by anyone, got that?"

Nadia's moment came soon after. Her mascara ran badly, and she was not delicate in wiping her eyes on the hem of her tunic. "These shoes!" she cried. "Does anyone have idea (Quack) how I hate them? I have pain to walk anywhere now, but (Quack) I cannot speak of it. No! No one cares!"

The older man leaned forward, solicitous through his tears. "But I care, Nadia. It (Quack) doesn't *matter*! You hear me? You're lovely (Quack) even without your 'fuck me' shoes."

"Where is my suite at Plaza Athenée, my penthouse on (Quack) Russian Hill? America gave me nothing! (Quack) Nothing! Just bad debts from dead husband, bad sex (quack) with marketing pipple like this boy's (Quack) brother, and shitty flat on Union Street. Now (Quack) I am nothing. Maybe is best. I hate America, yes, but not (Quack) from politics or such things as that. I hate the (Quack) happy hour, the blow-out sale, the MTV! You know? I am (Quack) hating the all-you-want-to-eat buffets. The popcorn. God, and the cinnamon! (Quack) Cinnamon in everything!"

Margot freed Brewster, first carefully peeling the tape from his chocolate-smeared face.

He took a deep breath. "Shall we have a little meeting in the hallway?" Once he'd extracted himself from the last of the tape, he calmly stepped into the bathroom, washed his face and brushed his teeth; he fetched his wallet and passport from his suitcase. He and Margot excused themselves, though the others barely noticed, immersed as they were in their very emotional, personal revelations, courtesy of MLII.

Outside the door, Margot reached out and gently touched the left side of Brewster's head. "You got a pretty good goose egg there. Not bleedin' much, but I bet it hurts like hell."

"Pretty much. Like a really bad localized hangover." He smiled weakly. "The chocolate was just as bad, honestly. But it could have been worse. Could have been Nestlé's Crunch."

She made a sympathetic noise. "So you slipped 'em some of your drugs from the League?"

"I did. But listen, we've got some quick decisions to make. We could call the *gendarmerie* right now, get them hauled in on a boatload of charges, and wait around to answer awkward questions about what happened to them. Depends on how vindictive you feel. Personally, I say we make a run for it. Right now. I'll leave all my things, I don't need any of it. You can get your bag and we'll get the next flight to somewhere else, what do you say?"

"I won't leave without at least calling Juliénas."

"You can do that once we get to the airport, get ticketed, and are close to boarding time. No one will be able to do much about stopping us then. How's that?"

They looked at each other for a moment.

"Shit, can you believe this? You bailed me out in a big way," said Margot, smiling almost shyly. He hadn't seen that look since he got her into the chateau dinner in Bordeaux more than two years earlier.

He chuckled. "Does it count that I was bound and gagged when I did it?"

Impulsively, she grabbed him in a bear hug. "I never told you this, but you always smell really good."

"I do?" He paused, hardly willing to believe she didn't have a punch line for a remark like that.

"It's true. Swear."

They pulled away and looked at each other again. Brewster was grinning. "Well, there *is* actually another option for us. We could step next door to your room for an hour or so. These people will still be—"

Margot laughed. "Brewster, you're the best." She gently brushed his hair off of his forehead. "Raincheck? Short term?"

"That," he said, dizzy with relief and elation, "is a deal. So shall we go in and say goodbye?"

"Are you serious?"

Brewster tapped gently on the door. When the older man responded, Brewster said, "Well, we're going to shove off. Thanks for everything. Why don't you folks call room service and enjoy a nice meal. My treat."

The fellow looked at him, wonderstruck. He reached out gently, patting Brewster on the shoulder. "Well that would be (Quack) just brilliant. And very kind of you, indeed, sir. Such a (Quack) good man."

"Try the *turbot*. It's excellent."

"Will do." Tears began to flow again. "I do so hate (Quack) goodbyes. It's (Quack) always very hard. Look after yourselves, will you?"

FLIGHT TO SOMEWHERE

By the time they had taken off on a United flight bound for Sao Paolo, Brewster had answered most of Margot's questions about what had happened. Information about their conversations is sketchy, since both were reluctant to talk in any detail; so I have had to rely primarily on remarks made to me by Don Fungibo in a 1994 phone interview, and on two junior college creative writing classes I took in 1971.

It was clear that the cluster bombs of adrenalin detonated during that day continued to reverberate.

"How'd you know we wouldn't both be killed right off the bat?" Margot said.

"I didn't. Which is why I wanted to get out of there right away. I guess the Univod guys were watching the Pauvrot pretty closely. But if we did get stuck there, my plan B was as good as any. What were we going to do, have a shootout? Overpower them?" He chuckled. "Too bad Heidi wasn't around. She'd have kicked the shit out of 'em."

He told her how lucky she was that she hadn't drunk any of the vodka in the glass that Nadia handed her, since he'd dusted all the glasses with the last of the Zipp/MLII combination he brought with him from Venezuela. "The bottle of Swillinger '78 was perfectly good, though. It was painful to leave it behind."

In the mad run-up to leaving Chuao for Paris, he had dosed two 500 milliliter bottles of Avion water that he had, as well as mini-size bottles of Insolent vodka, and Courmudgier cognac, all of which he brought to Paris in his suitcase. He didn't have enough ordnance to cover minis of whisky and other drinks, so he was counting on the water or the vodka minis to do the trick. And of course there were the dusted glasses as a backup.

"But how did you seal the Avion water bottles?" she said.

"That wasn't a big deal. The League trained all the operatives to use single unit closure equipment, for plastic and metal caps, too; I used it more than a few times—remind me to tell you about our operation against the Vomette Frères back in '87. Some of my best work. Actually, it wasn't long after we met. Anyway, all operatives had their own machines; I tossed mine into a box that went with me when I left San Francisco. I couldn't take the machine that caps bottles under pressure, like champagne or sparkling water—it was just too big and unwieldly. So I used what I had."

They did their best to relax in the seats of Expanded Quasi-Business Class, enjoying small bowls of cold mixed nuts with glasses of dry Oloroso sherry. Brewster held a cashew in his fingers, inspecting it. "I prefer the nuts warm, but that costs another two thousand dollars. A seat in True Business Class gets you warm nuts, not to mention a rose-bud vase on your tray table." He shrugged. "This sherry's very decent, I have to say."

"The ethyl acetate's pretty high, don't ya think? Makes the *rancio* a little crude."

"Oh, come on, Margot! Can't you just enjoy it?"

"Well fuck you, too. Pardon me for being observant."

He sighed. "Of course. Go for it. Don't mind me." He reached over and patted her on the knee. She put her hand on his.

When they had been in the air for more than eight hours, when they had had dinner and nearly two bottles of Numm's Prissy-les-Marne champagne to go with it, when the shades were down on the windows and only a few reading lights punctuated the shadowy cabin, Margot was huddled under a blanket with eyes closed and Brewster was leafing through a copy of Skymall Magazine. Margot slipped one arm out of her cocoon and nudged Brewster.

"I thought you were asleep," he said, looking up. "I was a little annoyed at you for being able to sleep with your mouth closed." He grinned.

"I can't sleep on these damn flights. It's like livin' inside a personal vibrator. I'm still too jacked up anyway."

"You want something to drink?"

"Nah." She turned to face him. "I'm feelin' kinda lost, Brewster. I mean, where am I goin'? What do I know about Venezuela? I've never been south of Tijuana."

"You think I'm taking you to a hell hole? Come on, Margot, I thought you were all about adventure."

"As long as the adventure doesn't get me killed."

His gaze sharpened. "So are you telling me you don't really want to be with me, is that it? Is this the moment when I have to say something like, 'I know you could learn to love me, just give it time'?"

She rolled her eyes. "There you go, pole-vaulting to conclusions again." Smiling and shaking her head, she said, "You can be such a jerk." She leaned in, put the flat of her palm on his shoulder and kissed him gently.

He pulled back and regarded her, gentle surprise in his eyes. "On the mouth! Heidi warned me about this stuff."

INTO THE JUNGLE

So what happened when Brewster returned to Chuao with Margot? We know that Margot was welcomed with open arms and small animal sacrifices by Don Fungibo, who in short order located her favorite eyeliner and explained that he could restore her hair to its natural color with just a few herbal treatments. "You promise I won't end up as a bald, naturalized Venezuelan witch?" she said with a laugh.

Margot plunged right into the cacao culture, soaking up information, applying her chemistry skills and legendary palate to the task of making great chocolate. Together, she and Brewster tasted scores of different dark chocolates from a dozen countries; in little more than a year her abilities exceeded Brewster's wildest imaginings, not to mention his own skills.

"So who's going to make the final call on this stuff? Ya know, when we don't agree," she said.

"What you mean is, is my male ego going to suffer?" said Brewster. "The answer to that is, I'm always willing to suffer for my art. And I have faith that you'll never fail to give me an appropriate raft of shit when necessary. Or let's say when you feel like it."

A less scrupulous author might recount rumors of their

marriage, and of Margot's pagan initiation into the cult of cacao at the hands of Don Fungibo himself. A less upright chronicler might, too, use titillating references to future adventures in a bid to create sequel-friendly momentum. These thrilling and potentially lucrative yarns, by the way, include fending off, in 1995, a ruthless band of chocolatier-terrorists attempting to steal their chocolate formulations. Who funded these *chocolatistas* is impossible to know with certainty; many believe it was Hershey, but an equal number accuse Nestlé. Others hold with the notion that it was the huge international vending machine conglomerate, Snackula LLC, bent on diabolical vertical integration.

Most challenging of all was Univod's international mass marketing, in 1996, of vodka-filled chocolates in the shape of a woman's face, offered in upscale gift boxes under the brand "Margot S." Dealing with that crisis made President Hugo Chavez's 1999 attempt to nationalize their plantation a comparative walk in the park. But these events are all outside the purview of this work, offering as they do the prospect of future book deals and their lifestyle-enhancing royalties.

It was in early 1994 that Don Fungibo negotiated a marketing deal with a well-known American chocolate manufacturer, an arrangement that would preserve the individuality of Brewster's products, to be sold under the Le Choc label. The first four small lots of chocolate hit the market in June of that year, and were an instant and stunning success. Each was from a unique planting of *criollo*, the most delicate and subtle of cacao beans. The exquisite flavor and undeniable snob appeal of such ultra-luxury chocolate created a sensation, bringing a flood of journalists, chefs, and foodies to the area, many of whom were willing to make the bruising trek into the mountains to find the plantation. Astonishingly, none of them ever saw Brewster or Margot. Rumors flew, of course. That Brewster and Margot weren't there, and never had been. That the plantation was run by a drug cartel. That the *brujo*, Don Fungibo, owned it, and was eventually going to sell it to Nestlé or Lindt, and use the money to retire to Miami and buy a chain of strip clubs. One explanation held that the two of them lived farther out in the mountains, in a hidden valley, and were visited only by locals who brought supplies and news about the increasing success of the chocolate.

But my favorite rumor, and the truest one, is that Brewster and Margot had an underground bunker built near the compound, to which they retreat when visitors approach. It is regularly stocked with luxuries imported at great expense; but it is worth it to both of them to have cases of nice wine, *foie gras*, charcuterie, good coffee, Badoix water, and other "necessities." They have good stores of their chocolate, too, of course, particularly the rarest and most exalted of the four, which is marketed under the name "Heart of Darkness." HOD, as it is referred to, needs no introduction for readers who haven't been living under a rock for the last fifteen years.

Because it's the most chic and expensive chocolate, the one they were proudest of, they made sure that a supply of HOD found its way to Juliénas and to the Bat. Brewster in particular was secretly delighted to learn that the San Francisco gourmet community was all atwitter about it, too, because that meant that Bernadette would have to try it. Would she know he and Margot had produced it?

Possibly, but even that didn't matter. What he loved most about the idea was the certainty that not only would she try it, but that she would love it. In spite of herself, she would love it.

APPENDIX I: WHERE ARE THEY NOW?

Back in San Francisco, the police located Carolyn just a day after Jock's death, in a suite at the Huntingford Hotel on Concave Hill. As I said, Brewster had been anxious to find her himself, for reasons not related to comforting her in her grief. He wanted the disks. Unfortunately, Nadia's high profile escape from the U.S. put the SFPD, and then the FBI, on alert. As one of her closest associates, Jock was bound to come under the microscope; and then there was the little issue of his death, under suspicious circumstances. Law enforcement had plenty of reason to turn his affairs inside out. Armed with warrants, they searched the house, found much Silver Tinkle data on the computer, and recovered the disks after questioning a shaken Carolyn. ("The natal charts of law enforcement officials are so often heavily configured in the fire triplicities, and in cardinal placements," she was heard to say. "I'm always so intimidated.")

The rest of Carolyn's story was curious enough.

Maybe not so surprisingly, she was in mourning for years, regretting the cruel and explosive final encounter with her husband. Was she too quick to judge? How could she have been so harsh toward the man she loved for so many years, a man with so many positive placements in his natal chart? She got in touch with a couple of spirit mediums who worked for Citigroup's commodity futures trading division and held weekly séances to attempt to locate Jock in the spirit world. They never made definitive contact, but after one of the early sessions, when the lights came up, there was a light dusting of orange powder on the table. One of the mediums swiped a delicate finger through it, put it to her lips and said, "Was somebody eating Cheezows? They were always a guilty pleasure for me, but that was years ago."

Carolyn coaxed Mum to attend a few sessions, but she said they seemed creepy. And after an hour she needed a smoke, anyway.

Initially, Mum was so crushed that she stayed in her room, day after day, and had Corinne bring her bowls of the housekeeper's famous milk chocolate oyster pudding, while she chain-smoked and listened to Sinatra, Andy Williams and Tony Bennett. Not only was Mum dealing with the loss of her elder son, but also of her company's CEO. Spodie International was adrift on the uncertain seas of commerce, without a skipper. It was only after Marvin came to see her one afternoon, a week after Jock's funeral, that fate gave a helping hand. In hindsight, it was obvious that Marvin would take over the CEO spot at Spodie, but it took their mutual interest in Gin Rummy to seal the deal.

Still in the habit of throwing I Ching hexagrams, he used what he saw as a particularly auspicious one, "Fun is easy/Convenience foods every night," to create Art on the Square. "Buy the art, get the wine free!" He was one of the first in the wine business to realize that original art was one of the few markets that attracted more stupid money than wine, or even fashion. So why not combine the two? He sold corrugated cases, hand-painted by a stoned-out collective in Sedona, for huge prices. Primitives on Cardboard, he called them. The wine itself hardly figured in the equation, and Spodie went on to make ten times its previous annual profits. The venture netted Marvin a nomination for the 1994 Nobel in Creative Marketing, though in the end he lost out to the creators of Beanie Babies.

He also masterminded another new product in the Spodie line of spirits, Cartel Tequila ("We bury the competition!"). Hugely popular by itself, it was an even more impressive juggernaut when coupled with his ingenious invention, the Margarita Pocket Aqualung, a joint venture with Spalding.

He ended up marrying Mum. They bought a huge ranch near Las Vegas, so she could take in all the shows, especially Wayne Newton and Engelbert Humperdinck; they also acquired a sea view villa in San Tropez, to allow Marvin to go barefoot and take surfing and sailboarding lessons. "Her smoking was tough to take at first. But she's pretty considerate about it," he said. He grinned. "And she really is a hot chick."

I would love to report that soon after her dosing at Brewster's hands, Nadia retired to a Ukrainian Russian Orthodox convent where she underwent a series of podiatric surgeries to relieve her pain, and where she now spends her days praying for the world's alcoholics. I would *like* to report that, but even I do not have the sack to try getting it past my readers, especially in this age of smart-bomb search engines. The truth is that only six months after being dosed, living on the run like a nomad, she attended a food and drink trade show in New York, where her emotional fragility, not to mention her looks, caught the attention of American food magnate Jeff Boyardee, who married her after a whirlwind tour of all Michelin three-star dance clubs in Western Europe. Tragically, they perished less than a year later, when their helicopter crashed on the way to a Metal concert on the isle of Minorca. Notices in the press were surprisingly sparse.

APPENDIX II: WHITHER VODKA?

And the status of vodka, what of that? There was a certain inevitability in how things unfolded. Inevitable, for example, that Univod should lose its grip on the world vodka market—a tribute to Margot and Brewster. Yet it did not lose its clout in Russia itself, and continues to be an *éminence grise*, the power behind all of Russia's governmental agencies and huge crony-capitalistic structure. You might insist that companies such as Gazprom, Lukoil, and Sberbank are the giants that turn the wheels of Russian life, but who's really in charge? As every Soviet leader from Stalin to Gorbachev has said: He who controls the vodka, controls Russia. Even the current leader of Russia, that famous dry drunk, accepts this as a reality and is careful to maintain a firm hand on the inner workings of Univod, attending the christenings of all children of its executives, as well as the annual Christmas party.

It was inevitable, too, that the formula guarded so zealously by what became known as the Latvian Junta would find its way into other hands—many other hands. Market forces would eventually prevail, finally achieving what sheer muscle or espionage could not, and what Brewster and Margot tried so valiantly to prevent. When the amount of money being offered reached a critical point, the Junta gave way, initiating sales of the formula to more than a dozen buyers. None of the resulting vodkas was identical to the original formula, of course, if only because each buyer ended up modifying his product with an eye toward besting the competition. So in effect the sale of the Silver Tinkle formula launched a thousand sips, a multitude of slight variations on the formula conceived by Jock and Nadia.

And so we arrive at the chaotic, crowded vodka market of 2006, which sees new ultra-premium products hit the market every year. Slickly packaged and brilliantly marketed, increasingly expensive and heavy with cachet, you will find them in the finest retail outlets, restaurants, shooting ranges, and mega-churches. The black label, the gold label, the red label, whatever—with flavor options expanding far beyond the old standbys of lemon, apple, mandarin orange, coriander, and barbeque beef, into new territory that includes crème brulée, horseradish, sevruga caviar, and Boston baked beans.

It's a little sad that the "new" vodkas should be having such a huge impact on the culture, since, as Margot would be quick to point out, the unflavored base products are not radically different in flavor characteristics—or lack thereof—from their predecessors. Or as she would say, "They're about as different as a handful of Number 8 wood screws." Yet there is no denying their influence when you consider the high profile historical events that have referenced them, from Unabomber Ted Kaczynski's request for a bottle of Blottoskaya "Purple Haze" when he was arrested in 1996, to Princess Diana's praise for Skyypee's Empyrean Kumquat, which she described as instrumental in getting her through her divorce.

On the other hand, you might be pleased to know that, in 2004, Blottoskaya's CEO and VP for Marketing were both dosed with a powerful new psychotropic substance, which at unpredictable moments reportedly induces loud and uncontrollable flatulence and a simultaneous compulsion to recite, in a loud voice, fictitious major league sports scores for hours at a time.

I comfort myself with the firm belief that Dion is still at his post, and that the League will endure.

CPSIA information can be obtained
at www.ICGtesting.com
Printed in the USA
LVHW030238071118
596099LV00001B/32/P